THE PLANE CRASHED—
AND THE CO-PILOT DIED!

Now Senator Ed Hill, who had piloted the plane, must face the Board of Inquiry to determine if he caused the accident. More than Hill's pilot's license is at stake. The Senator has been mentioned as a candidate for the vice-presidency, and a scandal would kill his chances. Steve Austin, who owes his rehabilitation to Senator Hill's support, must testify as an expert witness at his trial.

As the two sit in the flight simulator re-enacting the tragedy, Steve's problem grows. The Senator's version does not ring true. Yet the Senator is a good man; would he lie? Steve is an honest man; can he *honestly* absolve Hill of PILOT ERROR?

D1595775

Books In This Series

Six Million Dollar Man #1: Wine, Women and Wars
Six Million Dollar Man #2: Solid Gold Kidnapping
Six Million Dollar Man #3: High Crystal
Six Million Dollar Man #4: Pilot Error

Published by
WARNER PAPERBACK LIBRARY

ARE THERE WARNER PAPERBACKS
YOU WANT BUT CANNOT FIND IN YOUR LOCAL STORES?

You can get any Warner Paperback Library title in print. Simply send title and retail price, plus 25¢ to cover mailing and handling costs for each book desired. Enclose check or money order only, no cash please, to:

WARNER PAPERBACK LIBRARY
P.O. BOX 690
NEW YORK, N.Y. 10019

SIX MILLION DOLLAR MAN

#4
Pilot Error

A novel by
Jay Barbree

Based on the Universal Television Series
Created by Martin Caidin—Adapted from the episode
written by EDWARD J. LAKSO.

WARNER
PAPERBACK
LIBRARY

A Warner Communications Company

WARNER PAPERBACK LIBRARY EDITION
First Printing: August, 1975

Copyright © 1975 by MCA Publishing, a division of MCA, Inc.
All rights reserved

Cover illustration by John Mello

Warner Paperback Library is a division of Warner Books, Inc.,
75 Rockefeller Plaza, New York, N.Y. 10019.

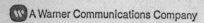 A Warner Communications Company

Printed in the United States of America

Not associated with Warner Press, Inc. of Anderson, Indiana

CHAPTER ONE

His left hand gripped the control yoke in a touch of caressing steel—firm, strong, yet with the gentleness born of years of flight, the knowledge and the touch that mark the pilot who becomes a part of his machine in its flight through the air ocean. Steve Austin kept his pressure on the yoke with his left hand. His right arm was extended slightly to his side, also extended forward, the fingers and hand grasping four parallel flat-sided knobs. The fingers were like those of a master musician, deft and dexterous, knowing that the slightest movement of those throttle knobs on the power quadrant could change the enormous flow of energy from four powerful turbofan engines. The engines were far from the men in the cockpit of the Boeing VC-135 transport, the military version of the famed 707 jetliner. Yet any movement of that right hand affected an entire stream of events.

Colonel Steve Austin kept his vision moving across the controls to the array of gauges on the instrument panel before him. He didn't *study* the gauges. You didn't do that because when you were flying a huge machine in a world of grayness you surveyed what was before you. Concentrate on one instrument, and you ignored the others. So you kept up a scan; your practiced eye picked out things that were wrong and paid scant or no attention to what was right.

It was no easy task at the moment, for the huge Boeing was in more than thick clouds. There was turbulence as well, shocks of air currents that slammed steadily into the airplane, that tossed it about and demanded full attention from its pilot. There was the tendency of the airplane to roll. The nose pitched up and down, and the shocks hammering along the great swept wings brought the nose yawing from side to side. There was no one movement, of course. It all took place simultaneously, so that the Boeing went through a constant series of motions that took place even as it hurtled through the cloud-filled night. Other motions were present, and they were felt by Austin as much as he could determine them from what he saw.

He needed no instruments to feel the trembling of metal as it flexed under the enormous pressures of flight through turbulence. The Boeing wing was an aeroflex design; it bent and twisted and curved under pressure, and the four engines in their big pods shuddered and moved up and down until the wing seemed to be alive. Which it was, of course. Metal flexing and bending and moving, and every motion carried through the great metal structure, transmitted to the control yoke, to the rudder pedals beneath Austin's feet, commanding instinctive and instant response on his part with the yoke and pedals and the throttles beneath his right hand. It was all a single motion made up of hundreds of tiny motions.

It was flight.

And it was a bad scene.

Trouble. Trouble in the form of an airplane that didn't *feel* right. Steve couldn't tell *what* was wrong, but the big airplane responded with less than the certain touch of power; it failed to answer the movements of his hands and his legs as he knew it should. He couldn't keep scanning the damned engine gauges the way instinct wanted him to do.

He had to *fly*. Fly the airplane, fly the avionics panels, checking navigation gauges, cross-checking airspeed with altitude and rate of climb and course

6

and homing needles. The sweepback of the big wing at thirty-five degrees made the Boeing less than the most stable airplane under this kind of turbulence. He had to concentrate on the *flying* of the big jet and rely upon the two other men with him in the flight deck to monitor the power systems. A swept wing had a bad disadvantage under certain conditions. If the nose yawed too sharply to one side, and the nose also rolled with a pitching motion, that sweepback could become fifty or even seventy degrees or more, and that meant one wing would stall out completely, the other would have almost no sweepback at all as the leading edge matched the forward movement of the airplane, and in an instant you could have an airplane with one wing devoid of lift and the other fully effective so that it acted as a huge aileron.

More than one ship like this one had been caught in such a situation, the violent rolling motion more than a pilot could handle, and in less time than it took to think about it the damned thing would be clawing over on its back.

So Steve Austin concentrated on the *now* of the moment and the flying. It mattered not one whit that he was also a man who had lived and performed and flown as an astronaut—indeed, as the last man ever to walk the surface of the moon when he commanded the Apollo 17 mission. None of that mattered. Only the *now* of flight. Only the *now* of not letting this big mother claw away from his grip. He was the maestro of a great orchestration of forces and movement, and as long as he kept that in mind he would remain master of the vessel he commanded.

To his right, in the copilot's seat, sat Ed Hill. Senator Edwin J. Hill, if you please. But he was a senator only when he wore his political garb. At the moment the word senator belonged somewhere a million miles away, because Hill was also in the Air Force Reserve, and when he donned Air Force blues he wore the single star on each shoulder of a brigadier general. At least twice a year he left his offices in Washington

7

and reported for active duty, put on his uniform, and went through the time-consuming and laborious procedures of being sure that he still knew what to do, and when, behind the controls of a large airplane with the star-and-bar insignia of the United States Air Force.

Tonight, despite his superior rank, he rode the right seat, and he was a general who was a copilot, and the man to his left, a colonel, was pilot and absolute commander of this winged vessel of the skies.

There was another man with them, Lieutenant Colonel Mark Dodson, flight engineer of the big VC-135 transport. Dodson sat in the flight engineer's seat behind the two pilots. He was utterly unconcerned with the problems faced by the two men in *flying* the machine. To Dodson the entire world was represented by his elaborate flight engineer's panel and the readings he saw on row upon row of instruments. Dodson was the stoker of the fires that fed power to the winged craft.

Until this moment he had even attended his own set of throttles. Up until this moment they had been in cruise configuration at 29,000 feet, and with the tender loving care of a man who *knows* his machinery on an intimate basis, Dodson had eked out perfect performance from the big engines. The gauges told him the engines were running the desired EPR of 2.38, which meant simply that the pressure of the air streaming hotly from the exhaust tubes of the engines was 2.38 times greater than the pressure of the air as it howled into the engines. EPR meant thrust, and thrust meant flight.

Within the engines the spinning of the compressors was down to a leisurely 8,500 revolutions per minute. Fuel consumption was normal. Indeed, it was calm compared to takeoff. When Austin rotated the nose upward the engines were sucking in fuel at more than 45,000 pounds per hour. That was the flow rate. At cruise they were down to about 12,000 pounds per

8

hour. Not bad. Six tons every hour to move the giant through the lower reaches of the stratosphere.

Dodson "saw" his engines with his mind's eye. He knew that the tailpipe temperature of each jet engine was more than 800 degrees Fahrenheit, that the super-heated air tearing away from each engine moved at more than 1,600 miles an hour. They—

"Time to initiate descent." Dodson glanced automatically to his left. That was General Hill's voice. As copilot he would call out each oncoming change in their flight operations. It was a safety procedure followed both by the miltiary and by the airlines.

Steve Austin glanced again through the instruments. They were at 29,000 feet and his flight plan called for bringing the Boeing to the ground in approximately twelve minutes from commencing descent.

General Hill called out the numbers. "DME reading nine zero miles to the runway."

"Right," Steve acknowledged. The Distance Measuring Equipment they called DME was giving them an automatic reading of distance to the airport. Austin planned to descend with an average true airspeed of 465 miles per hour. That would give them an average altitude drop of 2,500 feet per minute.

Steve kept the Boeing in clean configuration—gear, flaps, and spoilers retracted. His right hand tightened slightly on the throttle control knobs and eased them backward. General Hill was already in touch with RAPCON (Radar Approach Control) at Mason Air Force Base, clearing their descent, approach, and final switchover to the tower for landing. Behind Hill, Lieutenant Colonel Mark Dodson checked the fuel panel, made certain the main tank boost pumps were ON, and the center wing tank boost pumps were switched to OFF. He went through his checklist. Main tank number one fuel manifold valve to ON. All hydraulic quantity gauge readings were on the button. For the comfort of the crew and the pasengers in the long cabin behind them, Dodson moved quickly to keep cabin pressure commensurate with the descent.

9

He set the barometric correction on the cabin pressure control for the elevation of Mason Air Force Base and maintained a rate of change of cabin pressure to prevent a discomforting pressure buildup in the ears that could bring pain to them all. The way he had it set, four minutes before the VC-135 touched down the cabin would be at the same pressure elevation as the airfield.

Altitude fell away rapidly. Nose down, the great giant glided through the thick clouds, still rolling and pitching from the constant turbulence, the broad wings flexing and bending as they absorbed and cushioned the shock of air currents.

General Hill leaned back in his seat and motioned the flight engineer closer. He spoke quietly, close to Dodson's ear. The engineer gave him a startled look. His natural reaction to what he had heard from the general brought him to shake his head, a silent "No" to what he'd been told to do.

The general's face went stern. "Colonel, that is a direct order," he said.

Dodson nodded grimly. "Yes, sir."

Hill turned quickly. "Dammit, General, there's something *wrong* with this thing," Steve Austin was saying.

The general scanned the gauges. "She looks good, Steve," he said.

"I know, I know," the pilot answered slowly. "But I don't like the way she *feels*. I can't put my finger on it, but—"

General Hill nodded. If anyone knew how to fly the VC-135 it was Colonel Steve Austin. The airplane in its civil version had been flying long before Steve had ever climbed into the cockpit, but years later, as a test pilot at Edwards Air Force Base in California, Steve had performed accelerated dynamic stability tests with the VC-135 version. New engines, an extended fuselage, major modifications to internal systems and flap systems, all demanded the most intensive test program possible. After all, Air Force One, the same ship that was used to fly the President of the United

10

States throughout the country and the world, was the VC-135, and you didn't leave anything undone with such an aircraft. If anyone would be able to "feel" a wrongness in this machine, it would be Steve.

"Dodson, how's the power holding?"

The flight engineer turned his head. He hesitated a moment before answering. "Everything's in the green, sir."

"Roger." Steve frowned. He just couldn't put his finger on it. Well, he told himself, fly the damn thing, that's all. The rate of descent was off. They'd been coming down just a tad too fast. It didn't seem like much, but there wasn't any reason for an accelerated descent. Not with everything where it belonged. Steve stayed busy, fighting the turbulence, checking the flight panel automatically. The general called out position fixes and performance readings in a comfortable monotone.

Still far out from the airfield, Steve held the VC-135 in a wide, gentle bank. RAPCON had a clear scope blip from the transponder in the airplane, and Steve listened without comment to the conversation between General Hill and the ground controllers. Except for that disconcerting uneasiness, Steve felt it was an ordinary descent.

He rode her down on the gauges, eating away the miles and altitude. Well, whatever was wrong, it was all being set up for an easy approach. If you could call fighting worsening turbulence easy, which was a fault of oldtime pilots, who tended to stay unflappable in all but the worst weather.

Watching the gauges, listening to Hill's conversation and his call-outs, Steve set up the Boeing for a long downwind leg into Mason Air Force Base.

"Flaps thirty degrees," Steve called.

Hill grasped the flap handle, moved it back, and locked it in the thirty-degree position. When the indicator dial showed the flaps at their desired position, he called out the numbers. "Flaps, thirty degrees." During the lowering of the flaps at the wing trailing edge,

11

another control surface moved automatically into position. As the massive flaps slid down and backward, passing the position of nine and a half degrees, hydraulic arms extended leading edge flaps from the front edge of the wing. The airflow changed across the wing, and abruptly the low-speed sensitivity and control of the Boeing improved to a marked degree.

"Leading edge flaps out," Hill called, then, moments later, "Outboard ailerons free." In high-speed flight, the outboard ailerons of the VC-135 locked into position as part of the wing. At low speed and with flaps extended, the ailerons again came "alive," and Steve had two sets of ailerons on each wing under his control.

The airspeed indicator showed 240.

Then, they were below 200 miles per hour.

Steve called it out. "Gear down."

Hill worked the lever. Beneath the fuselage huge doors snapped open, and a shock rumbled through the VC-135. Six seconds later the nose gear was down and locked. Three seconds more and the massive eight-wheeled main gear was down and locked.

"Three in the green," announced Hill.

"Right. Three green," Steve replied.

But his frown had deepened. The speed was dropping and—

"*Watch your airspeed.*" A sudden sharp tone from General Hill.

Damn, she was getting mushy. Steve's right hand went forward on the throttles. There came a meaningful reply, audible, a rich-throated whine as he fed in power. But still she was too slow!

"Airspeed! *You're thirty low!*"

Steve rammed the throttles full forward. He could gain airspeed by dropping the nose even more, but there were steep hills below them in the fog, and they were almost at minimum descent altitude.

"Altitude two thousand six hu—"

Steve broke in, his words snapped out. "Give me MDA."

"You're at it. MDA two thousand five hundred. Runway twenty-one hundred." His voice went tight. "You're at two thousand four hundred. One hundred feet below MDA. Bring her up!"

Steve cursed to himself, going for maximum power.

"Two hundred feet below MDA!"

She wouldn't respond fast enough. She just wasn't coming around and— Steve broke into his own thoughts. "Flaps to takeoff!" he snapped. "Go-around!"

He was aborting the approach. Everything was getting out of hand. They were sinking like a rock. The airspeed needle was still dropping. They were too low, too slow, and he had full power, the engines screaming, and she wasn't coming around fast enough. A sudden shock of turbulence whipped one wing up, and the big airplane was shuddering. Red lights flashed on the panel and—

"You're losing her! Bring in everything she's got!"

Damn! He didn't need the general's voice barking in his ear. He knew damned well what was wrong.

"Gear coming up." Hill was calmer now, calling it out.

"Flaps at takeoff setting. *You're still too slow.*"

He knew that . . .

The speed was falling off. He fought to level the wings, but the big airplane responded with maddening slowness, the controls mushy. His right hand jammed against the throttle knobs.

"*You're losing her!*" Hill's voice was shrill.

He had no choice. He had to lower the nose. The cockpit shook wildly as the Boeing rumbled violently on the edge of a stall. Steve went forward on the yoke, the power full on, engines screaming, and—

Blurred shapes before his eyes. Hill's voice, in a shout. "*We're going to hit!*"

A tremendous explosion ripped through the cockpit. Something exploded, filling the world with light. They were tossed about violently in their straps and . . .

13

The voice came from a distance, as though it were filtered from far away. It had a slight mocking tone.

"Gentlemen, you have just crashed."

Steve looked at the general, who stared back, white-faced.

The voice continued, *"It is my sad duty to inform you that everyone aboard this aircraft is dead."*

The lights went out.

CHAPTER TWO

The lights came on slowly. General Hill leaned back in his seat. His hands shook as he lit a cigarette and sucked in deeply. He waited several moments before speaking.

"These things always scare the hell out of me. They're just too damned realistic."

Steve stared straight ahead. He released his shoulder harness and seat belt. "Freeze the gauges, please," he ordered to his invisible audience.

The computer controller of the elaborate, painfully realistic flight simulator responded at once. "Yes, sir. All gauges frozen. Flight recorders are stopped. The tapes will be available for your review in just a few minutes, Colonel."

It was the same filtered voice that had announced the crash and told them they had all been killed in the impact.

Steve turned finally from the instrument panel to the man at his right. General Hill gestured with his cigarette. There was a look of complete vindication on his face.

"Now you know what it was like, Colonel. What it was like that night coming into Luke Air Force Base." He sucked deeply on the cigarette. The color was still returning slowly to his face. When you "crashed" in one of these flight simulators you went through the "real thing." It grabbed you right in the gut. More often than not, you were so preoccupied you forgot you were in the damned simulator.

"The only difference," continued Hill, "was that I was sitting where you are now. The left seat."

The general's face went harsh. "There was one other difference, of course. That crash was *real*."

Steve nodded slowly. He knew all that. He knew that the general had been flying a VC-135, that he'd descended toward Luke, and that something went wrong, terribly wrong, and the Boeing had slammed into the ground short of the runway, stalling, shaking viciously before it hammered against the earth.

Steve looked steadily at the general. "It just doesn't make sense. I flew this thing by the numbers. All the way. And, General, there's just no way this airplane can stall out like we did with the speed and the power we had going." He glanced upward, an automatic reflex for the controller he couldn't see.

"Sergeant, did we have any problems with the spoilers? Something that might not have shown on the gauges?"

The spoilers, deploying at the wrong moment, would have drastically destroyed the lift of the wing. "No, sir. Everything was right on the money with the spoilers, Colonel."

Steve rubbed his chin. "And yet we didn't have the speed we needed."

"Right," General Hill confirmed. "And we crashed. And I have a date with a Board of Inquiry from the Air Inspector General's office to explain why an airplane I was flying crashed, and why four people out of eleven in my crew were killed."

He studied Steve Austin carefully. "Dammit, Colonel, you were one of the lead test pilots on this machine. Haven't you figured it yet?"

"You're setting me up," Steve said warily.

"Damned right I am," Hill responded, not even trying to conceal the heat within him. "Because *I've* been set up, and I have no intention of taking the

16

hammer for something that I'm being blamed for—
not when the blame isn't mine."

"Well, we know it wasn't the spoilers. What about
the flap settings? If we had an indication of leading
edge flaps but they weren't really extended. Wait a
moment," he interrupted himself, "remember that first
fatal crash in the 747, in Africa? That was on takeoff.
The aircraft got about a hundred feet off the ground
and then settled back in and crashed. It turned out
they had full power and the leading edge flap indicator
was in the green, but the flaps had never extended.
If that happened to us then—"

"Sir." It was the simulator controller's voice. "I've
been monitoring your conversation. No problem with
the flaps, Colonel Austin. They were green and they
were out."

Steve looked again at the general by his side. "Then
it *could* have been power. We were slow to respond.
But all gauges showed—" He turned to the flight
engineer. "Dodson, I had full throttle. You didn't
call any engines out or—"

General Hill glanced at the flight engineer. "Don't
answer that."

Steve showed his surprise. "And why the hell not?"
he demanded.

"Dammit, Austin, work it out yourself like you're
doing."

Steve stared at the engine gauges on the panel.
Everything was in the green. He turned to the flight
engineer's panel. Dodson moved aside.

One gauge leaped out at Steve.

"Number four engine! *It was out!*"

General Hill laughed without humor. "Welcome to
the club, Colonel."

"I don't understand you." Steve was angry, and he
wasn't bothering to conceal it. "You don't cover up an
engine-out condition, dammit. General, I don't care
who you—"

"Just hold it right there," General Hill snapped at
him. "The purpose of this little exercise wasn't to

17

test *you*, Austin. It was to duplicate what happened to me that night at Luke when I was sitting in your seat. *And when my copilot didn't call out a dead engine for me before I crashed.*"

A long pause followed. Several times Steve started to respond, and each time he clamped his lips tight. His expression and his words were more guarded when finally he broke his silence. "I see," he said slowly, and it was obvious he now had less than complete trust in the man by his side. "So that's why you set this up in the simulator the way you did. Before I would be called in to testify."

"Exactly," Hill told him. "I wanted you to go through the whole thing—to *know* what it was like—before you step into that witness box."

Steve shook his head slowly. "There's more to it than that, General. What about your copilot? What about *his* story? He won't be telling his story, will he? But I happened to know Tom Jeffers for years. I flew with him. He was one of the best. And let me add, General, he wasn't the kind of man who'd screw up on his pilot by *not* calling out an engine problem."

"You're right, of course," Hill said quickly. "He was one of the best. He was also an honest man. And he'd be the first to admit—to explain what happened, that he made a mistake."

Steve rose slowly from his seat and stepped back in the simulator cockpit. He stopped and looked directly at the general. "Too bad he won't be able to do that, isn't it?"

Hill gestured angrily for Steve to stop right where he was. "Look, Colonel, I knew Tom just as long as you did. He *was* one of the best. I don't need to pass off the *blame* for what happened on a dead man. All I want on that witness stand is the *truth*."

They locked eyes. Emotions played across their faces. "Of course, Senator."

It was the first time Steve had referred to Hill as anything except "General."

"Excuse me, sir." He brushed his way past the other man and left the simulator.

Senator—and General—Edwin J. Hill showed honest pain on his face. He shook his head sadly before following.

Lieutenant Colonel Dodson swore under his breath.

Outside the simulator, pacing impatiently beneath the harsh sun, a tall, angry figure had waited for more than an hour for the "flight" to reach its inevitable conclusion. Joe Lannon had worked for Ed Hill for years, since his first congressional term. He'd been his administrative assistant all that time. He was an expert at political infighting and a tough tackle leading the way through many of the roughest political battles Ed Hill had ever fought. In many ways, Hill was a senator because of the talent, guidance, and tough battling of this man. Hill was on several powerful committees in Washington, and no one knew better than did Joe Lannon that the Air Force investigation of the crash, if it showed incompetence on the part of Senator Edwin J. Hill while he was on temporary active duty, could wreck many of the plans that he'd worked for years to bring to pass.

Lannon looked about suddenly as Steve Austin emerged from the simulator. He showed no sign of recognition as he passed Lannon, but strode away quickly. A moment later Hill appeared. Lannon threw him a shrewd, questioning look, but the senator ignored his aide and hurried after Austin. Steve looked to his side as Hill joined him and matched his stride.

Hill took a deep breath. "Dammit, Steve, I'm not playing any political games, and I'm not asking any favors. For God's sake, man, I don't want you beggaring the truth! And that's exactly what I told you in there. The *truth.*"

Steve nodded slowly, never slowing his stride. "Senator, I don't question your word. Do you believe that?"

"Yes. Yes, I do."

"But dammit, sir, I feel . . . Look, Senator, you'll

19

have to forgive my feelings at the moment. I don't like being 'used.' And that's just what you've been doing with me."

"I admit that," Hill told him frankly. "But it was the only way to get the truth to you without saying it only in words. I'm telling you that number-four engine was out. Long before we hit the ground. When I initiated the go-around, coming into Luke, I played that airplane as though I had full power. Which I believed, as God is my witness, that I did. It's all in the accident report. You'll be able to see it for yourself. The flight recorder they recovered from the wreckage *proves* it. You don't even have to take my word for it."

He lit another cigarette as they walked. "There's more to it than justifying my competence as a pilot, Colonel." Hill took a long drag on the cigarette and exhaled noisily. "The facts are that I'm a United States Senator. I'm a reserve general officer in the United States Air Force." He touched Steve's arm, and they stopped.

"But above all else, and I'm being as honest with you as I know how, Steve, *I'm a pilot*. Even if it's just as a weekend warrior in the reserve right now. I didn't get here on any political sled. I came up through the ranks. I—"

Steve broke in, a tight smile on his face. "I'm the last one to knock the weekend warrior, General. Don't forget that's my status also."

Hill nodded, his face grave. "All right, then you understand even better than I can say it. When you're on reserve flying status, you tend to be extra careful. You've *got* to be that much more careful. You can't screw up. You *work* for the proficiency check every six months. And I did that. I worked at it. And I was *ready* for it. Mentally, and physically. Dammit, Steve, if Tom Jeffers had said one word, *just one word* about that engine, I would have done what was necessary, compensated for it, done what I should have done. Can you believe that?"

20

Steve looked at the other man and hesitated before answering. His reply was worded carefully, and he wasn't harsh in his response. "Look, Senator," he said quietly. "I'm not your judge. I'm not and I don't want to be. Believe me when I tell you that. I was a test pilot in a test program on this airplane, so they've called me back as an expert witness. I didn't want any part of this, and I wish I weren't involved now. I happen to hold you in some pretty high respect, and the whole thing is uncomfortable to me. But I'm also on duty, and I'm wearing the blue suit because I've been ordered to. Just like I've been ordered to testify. I'll do just that. I'll testify as to the performance of the aircraft, *not* the man inside it. And I'll try to be as honest as I can without involving personalities. Dead or alive. Is that laying it out the way you want to hear it?"

Hill chewed his lower lip. "All right," he said, nodding. "That's fair enough."

"Then I'll see you at the field tomorrow." Hill watched Steve Austin walk away.

Joe Lannon came up slowly from behind. "Well, Senator, let me have it straight. Is he with us or against us?"

Hill gave him a humorless smile. "Poor Joe," he said, shaking his head. "Is that the only way you can see people? You're looking at an honest man. Steve Austin isn't for *or* against. He's going to tell the truth. He'll tell it the way he sees it. And that's all I can ever ask from any man." He slapped Lannon on the back.

"And I don't see any way the truth can hurt me, right?"

Lannon hesitated. He didn't like any of this. Things were never *that* cut and dried. He wanted better control of what was happening. There was the barest cutting edge to his voice. "No . . . of course not. The truth. That's what we all want."

21

CHAPTER THREE

The cool breeze brought to him the clean taste of the Pacific in early morning. His eyes looked across Lindbergh Field's concrete strips pointing to a thousand other worlds. The sound came to Senator Edwin J. Hill first as a whisper, but his recognition was immediate. It was the mounting cry of a 727 jetliner standing at runway's end, preparing to hurl itself down the ribboned concrete. Senator Hill tensed to the sound, listening as the roar swelled in volume. The jet was rolling. He turned, and the 727 came into view. He watched as the sleek machine thundered by, as the pilot rotated and the jet clawed its way into the sky. He felt comfortable. It was like looking through a window into your home.

He stood by a blue-and-yellow Navion with the figures 4372 and the letter K painted on its fuselage. It was his plane. His ticket to that world known only and guarded jealously by the pilot breed. Oh, he was a weekend warrior, right enough. One of the thousands of reserve pilots who receive their rationed hops into the air from the military. But a real airman needed a continuity in his flights as much as an addict needed his daily fix. And, Ed Hill reminded himself, the only way you get that is with your own plane.

He checked his person, reassuring himself his Air Force dress blues were pressed and sharp, befitting the star he wore on each shoulder. This morning he was again Brigadier General Edwin J. Hill. Not U.S. Senator Edwin J. Hill. He was the first in his party to arrive at Lindbergh Field, to wait for the aircraft that was to take them to the hearing at Luke Air Force Base where a panel of men could, on the slightest whim, pluck his flight world from his grasp like hungry chickens fighting over the last grain of corn.

He frowned at the sudden thought of losing even his Navion. Not only was his Air Force flight status threatened by the crash at Luke, but those yahoos could see to it he was grounded, period. Even from private flying.

Well, that damn well wasn't going to happen. Not after yesterday's simulator ride with Colonel Steve Austin, the last man to walk on the moon, a national hero and, he managed a comfortable smile, one of the best test pilots to ever land his share of cranky machines on the desert at Edwards. Hell, he swore, what better man could I have testifying to *what* happened?

Hill breathed deeply, feeling renewed confidence in what he must face this day as he waved to a lanky youth getting out of a car a short distance away. His seventeen-year-old son, Greg, had arrived for the trip to Luke. Hill was not at all surprised that he found himself wondering why. Ashamedly, he knew he and Greg hadn't been all that close in recent years, and he faulted no one but himself. A U.S. Senator's life leaves damn precious little time for anyone, especially family. When it came to his wife, Janice, this did not bother him too much. But Greg? Well, that was another matter altogether.

He watched his son walk toward him, knowing Greg did not share his love for flight. Nevertheless, he could not help wondering why Greg had chosen medical school instead of a field closely aligned with his. He wondered, but he did not deny his son's right to follow his own path. He had given him a good home, would give him a good education, and though Greg might feel otherwise, all the love he could muster.

23

"Glad you could make it, son," he greeted Greg, putting an arm across the lad's shoulders.

Greg sat his overnight bag on the concrete beside his father's and pointed to the Navion. "You really love that old bird, don't you, Dad?"

"Uh-huh. Still keep my fishing gear in the back." He smiled, facing Greg. "Can you keep a secret, son?" he asked. "I flew her around the pattern this morning."

"Good for you, Dad," Greg said, returning the smile. "She's a great-looking ship."

"She's that," Hill agreed, watching his son touch the Navion softly.

They walked around the aircraft together, and Hill sensed his son's admiration for the old plane. The lad's kinship for the Navion made him feel warm inside, although he knew Greg's lack of fondness for flying. Hill also knew few people realized just how great the Navion really was. For years it had been the subject of much love and affection and had had dozens of extensive modifications performed on it, including modification to a twin.

And when it came to comfort, newer aircraft were forced into a back seat. The Navion is wider than anything still in production, and your legs dangle off soft, well-shaped seats that make cross-countries an exercise in easy living. And when it comes to visibility, Hill mused to himself, none can match it. The noise level is just as great. At climb power conversation isn't hard at all. Level her out and ease back the power, and the noise level is lower than some of your better made cars. As a luxury cruiser, the Navion, which has a range in excess of 1,500 miles, is hard to beat.

Hill turned to see Greg looking down the long row of planes, his son's eyes moving along winged shapes of all sizes, including some of World War II vintage.

"Want to take a closer look, son?" he asked, gesturing toward the row of parked aircraft.

"Sure, Dad, whatever you say," Greg replied, following his father toward the planes, where the senator began with a running, unbroken description of what

24

the planes were. The lad paid scant attention to the sleek new shapes. He bent beneath the wings of old fighters and a few bombers that had been salvaged and kept flyable by men who had flown in past wars. They had names Greg had heard only dimly in conversations when his father talked with other pilots of an air age that seemed to him to have been lost forever. Not here, the young man realized, as his father took him around and into the shapes that assumed personalities as his hand caressed the metal.

Greg was dragged in and out of cockpits and watched his father wallop a fist against the engine nacelle of a gleaming B-25 while making rude noises about the gliding angle of a hulking Avenger and looking fondly at a Hellcat. He lost track of the names, but his father knew them all, intimately; he knew their vices and he sang their praises and he was drunk with the graceful shapes, weary and worn as they were.

They continued their movemnt in and around the aircraft, and Greg found himself admiring his father's enthusiasm for the old planes, recalling a time when he too enjoyed such love for the winged creatures. But that had been early in his seventeen years. One day in particular in the summer when he was six years old.

An Old Country Style Air Show they called it. And he could remember clearly how he sat by his father, wriggling with wild excitement as a gaudily checkered biplane roared past the stands directly before them. The figure of a man in a bright orange suit and yellow helmet showed clearly above the top wing. Feet spread wide and clothes snapping with the wind, leaning into the wire braces anchoring him to the upper wing, the man waved. And Greg was certain the "wing walker" had waved just to him.

It was a beautiful day, the rich blue sky flecked with cumulus and washed in sunlight. A pleasant breeze carried away the heat. All about them festivity reigned at the air show—laughing barnstormers turning the clock far back from the summer of 1964. For Greg it

25

was one of those special days when he was alone with his father, doing things together . . .

A snarl crashed over them as the biplane pilot sucked up the nose. The crowd roared and shrieked along with Greg as the wheels of the airplane skimmed the grass and then lifted skyward. The nose went up and color flashed brilliantly in its checkered pattern as the wings came around, rolling toward them.

"Watch carefully, son," his father had said. "He's going to roll her all the way around."

It didn't seem possible for Greg's wide eyes to open more, but they did.

"Daddy, he can't," Greg protested, throwing his arms around his father's neck, holding tightly. "The man will fall!"

"No; just watch."

The nose rotated more and the biplane swooped upward, on her back, the wire-braced figure waving harder than ever. A hush shot through the stands as the pilot hauled back on the stick, kicked in rudder, stopped the roll, and brought the biplane out into a climbing turn.

No sooner than the "wing walker" atop the biplane had slipped from their view, Greg's attention was captured by something else. High overhead a tiny dot swelled in size, trailing a thickening plume of bright red smoke. Seconds later two other planes flashed in low, one from each side of the stands, the pilots horsing their agile machines straight up, rolling, giving a corkscrew effect to their smoke. The three planes joined and swept as one over the field, trailing their smoky banner of red, white, and blue.

It was a day remembered easily by Greg, who recalled, in detail, all the air show's heart-thumping flying, his pleasure in being a spectator. It wasn't until the air show was over that, even then at six years old, he realized the enjoyment had been in watching, not in participating.

As the crowd thinned from the stands, his father had dragged him bubbling and smiling to a nearby airplane which belonged to one of his friends. Greg had never seen an airplane like it before. It could only be a fighter. Suddenly the smile left his face as he stood beside the gleaming red-and-white machine, staring at the huge propeller, the long curving canopy.

"Daddy, what is it?"

"Mustang."

"Is—is it a fighter airplane, Daddy?" the boy looked up. "It looks mean."

His father nodded. "Know how many seats it has?"

The boy shook his head.

His father held up two fingers. "Just enough for the two of us, son," he smiled. "I'm gonna take you up for a ride. Up there," he pointed toward the sky.

"But, Daddy . . . !"

It was too late. The boy felt his father's arms lift him upward, and a few minutes later he felt numb. He felt webbed, tied, and trussed up in the rear seat of the Mustang. His father fastened his seat belt, inserted the shoulder harness into its mechanism and yanked the boy so tightly he couldn't move. He showed the boy—or directed his hand, he couldn't see—a small ratchet handle along his left thigh and told the boy how to move the handle so that he could release the tension on the shoulder harness and have some comfort in flight. Greg was ready to climb out of the Mustang when his father placed a leather helmet over his head and plugged in several electrical connectors.

"Earphones in the helmet," his father shouted. "I'll leave it plugged in so you can talk to me anytime you want."

The boy grasped a soft rubbery thing hanging to the side of the helmet. "What's this, Daddy?"

"Oxygen mask. When you want to talk to me, just hold it close to your face. This doohickey here holds the microphone. You won't be needing oxygen; this thing is pressurized. Got it?"

Greg closed his eyes tightly and shook his head.

27

"Good boy," his father said, leaning over into the cockpit to pat him on the back.

Greg gritted teeth as he watched his father move forward on the wing to climb into the front seat.

"How do you read me, son?"

Only the seat belt and shoulder harness kept him from leaping forward. "W-what?" Then he remembered; the earphones. He pulled the mask close to his face.

"Is that you, Daddy?"

"Right, son," his father's voice came through the earphones. "Hold on tight, here we go."

The Mustang trembled as the huge propeller jerked around, then caught with a booming thunder. Greg watched the instrument gauges, recognizing only a couple with which he had become familiar from flights he'd taken with his father in smaller airplanes. Beyond his father's head and shoulders he saw only a long metal nose and the blur of the propeller. He listened to the exchange between his father and the tower and tensed as he heard ". . . cleared to taxi into position and hold." Thunder increased, and the lean and hungry fighter swung onto the runway, rocking gently as his father applied the brakes.

"Mustang six seven hotel cleared for takeoff."

"Roger."

Then to Greg. "All set, son?"

"Yes—yessir," he mumbled into the mask.

Greg watched the throttle to his left moving steadily forward as his father fed power to the engine. For several seconds the Mustang moved forward with a steady pace. Then she seemed to rise as he brought up the tail. The wings level now with the runway, his father went to full power. The roar crashed through the airplane, and Greg was mashed back into his seat. He couldn't believe the sudden rush down the runway; everything was happening so fast! The stick came back. Greg could see now, buildings blurring as they flashed by them. Suddenly the nose lifted, he felt the thump of the gear coming up beneath him, and the

28

world became a blur of clouds and sunlight as his father brought the fighter up into a howling climb to the left.

Greg began to collect his senses after his father eased out of the climb and leveled off. The earth drifted far below them. He stared at the altimeter: 22,000 feet. He asked his father their speed.

"Got us a nice wind helping us up here, son," the voice came through the earphones. "Our ground speed is about three-ninety."

"Three hundred and ninety miles an hour?"

"Right, son. Sit back and enjoy it."

Greg didn't talk for a while. The intense deep blue—almost a dark purple—of the sky directly overhead swept through him, deepening his loneliness. It was almost as if they were leaving the world behind, cutting themselves forever loose from earth. The boy felt so helpless. Everything had happened with such a rush that his thoughts still whirled.

"Are you ready for some real flying, son?" his father asked, his voice drunk with delight.

"Yes, I—I guess so, Daddy."

A loud yell burst from the earphones and the sky whirled crazily in a blur of sun and clouds and horizon. Greg felt his small body grow quickly heavy against the seat. Then, just as quickly, he was floating, and dizziness swept through his brain, his stomach churning to get rid of the hot dogs, the Cokes, the cotton candy he had consumed at the air show. He wanted desperately to be done with it, to be home where he could feel his feet on earth, the safety of his own bed. But there was nothing he could do but shut his eyes, grip his seat, and bear what was a growing fear far beyond his wildest nightmare.

His father was drunk with the sensation of flight, with the response from the Mustang through one maneuver after the other. And when it was finally over, and they had landed, Greg realized he had not opened his eyes since he closed them at 22,000 feet.

Greg studied his father standing on the wing of another Mustang, leaning into the cockpit with a broad grin. Their tour of the flight line had halted when they reached the old fighter. Now, Greg stood shaking his head, smiling. Eleven years after his *only* flight in one of the lean Mustangs, nothing had changed. Not that he expected it, or really wanted it to change. He understood his father's obsession with flight, in fact admired it in many ways. Certainly more so than most facets of *Senator* Edwin J. Hill's life.

It wasn't his father's flying that bothered him. It was the politics, the restrictions of being the son of a prominent political figure. Well, that would matter little after medical school. He would slip quietly into a life of helping others, unnoticed.

In a way he was doing just that, now. Helping his father at a time when he was needed. He was not unaware of what the Board of Inquiry could do to Edwin J. Hill, the pilot. And, suddenly, seeing his father's moment of contentment with the old World War II fighter, Greg was pleased that he was going along on the trip to Luke. He started toward his father to tell him so when his attention was diverted by a shout.

"Hey, Ed! What the hell are you doing?"

Greg saw Joe Lannon, his father's aide, coming toward them with obvious distaste for the Mustang.

"Good morning, Joe." Hill waved, moving down from the wing. "You know what this is? It's a Mustang, rebuilt and as clean as a whistle, Joe."

"It's a piece of junk, Ed," Lannon snapped. "What the hell are you doing here in this—this museum, anyway?"

"Just waiting on you, Joe," the Senator explained. "Greg and I were just passing the time."

"Uh-huh, sure," Lannon frowned. "Now look at your dress blues," he scolded, moving his hands about Hill's uniform, checking the garment for dirt. "And look at your shoes, Ed!" he pointed. "They're all scuffed up."

30

"Awright, awright, Joe," Hill waved him away. "Forget the mother hen routine," he ordered his aide, taking a handkerchief from his pocket before bending down to polish his shoes until they had a new shine. "See, Joe," he said, looking up. "No problems. Everything is gonna be just fine. Right?"

"Hell, I hope so, Ed," Lannon moaned. "This Board of Inquiry won't be a piece of cake. And besides that," he gestured over his shoulder, "the reporters are waiting."

"Where?"

"I got 'em set up in the Executive Aircraft Terminal," Lannon explained. "Told 'em you'd hold a press conference."

Senator Hill raised a hand, smiling. "Lead on, Joe," he said. "I told you, today we have no problems."

"We'll see," Lannon snapped, turning abruptly to walk across the concrete apron with quick, sharp strides.

Senator Hill and Greg followed the man, struggling to keep pace until they reached the terminal, where Lannon stopped just long enough to make another brief inspection of Hill's uniform before moving quickly through the door.

Inside, facing them, were batteries of blinding floodlights, stabbing cruelly into their eyes. The lights accented thick clouds of smoke and, in between and at the bottom of the smoke, a sea of faces and gesticulating arms dissolved into a bed of unreal creatures writhing about and pouring forth an avalanche of sound.

For Greg, it was an unnerving scene, and he stopped suddenly, raising a hand to shield his eyes from the glare. He watched his father and Joe Lannon move through the crowded room to face the reporters.

"May I have your attention, please?" Greg heard Joe Lannon ask as he held up a palm. The voices fell away, and Greg was impressed with Lannon's ability to assume some control of the undisciplined gathering.

31

"Senator Hill just arrived, and he's here to answer any and all of your questions." Lannon stepped aside, motioning to Hill. "Senator."

The momentary quiet proved to be just that, and Greg was startled to see the group of reporters leap to their feet all shouting questions, engulfing his father with flashing, eye-stabbing cameras, with microphones and pads. He watched with mouth open as they shouted, jostling and pushing, and he jumped frantically when a voice shouted at him from behind. "Hey, kid, over here."

At first he pretended not to hear, but quickly he felt a hand grab his shoulder. "You're Senator Hill's son, aren't you?" he heard a woman ask.

He turned to see a wide-eyed creature. "That's right, Greg Hill," he answered in a whisper.

"Greg?"

"Yes, ma'am."

"Greg, whatta you think about your father appearing before the Board of Inquiry? What are his chances?"

"I don't know, I—" He never finished his answer. A microphone smacked against his cheek, and the flashes of light made him cringe. He gasped as a photographer leaped suddenly to a nearby table, trying for a higher shot, aiming his camera down over the heads of the mob surrounding his father.

There were hands and the lights and voices shouting and yelling and Greg saw two other men standing on another table, waving for his father to look toward their cameras. It was a nightmarish scene and Greg stood rigid amid the chaos surrounding him.

It seemed like hours, but only minutes had passed when he was aware that the onslaught of ill tempers and bad manners had been brought under control by the cool, professional touch of Senator Edwin J. Hill at work. Greg always forgot just how good his father was at his job. He watched admiringly and when it appeared the press conference was ending, he moved through the group of reporters to his father's side.

"Well, gentlemen, my son and I have a long flight

ahead of us," he heard his father say. "If there are no further questions—"

"One moment, Senator," a reporter spoke behind the crowd, waving *her* arm for attention. "There are reporters here who are not *gentlemen*," she said with a touch of acid. "I have another question."

"Of course." Hill blushed. "You must forgive me. One gets accustomed to—"

"I understand only *too* well," she interrupted. "My question is," the reporter continued, "do you feel this inquiry is an attempt to embarrass you politically?"

"Oh no, not at all," Hill assured the reporter. "I was the pilot in command on that tragic day. This is my opportunity to prove that I lived up to the highest traditions of that responsibility."

"Responsible enough to be nominated as your party's next Vice Presidential candidate?" the reporter asked with a touch of sarcasm.

Hill smiled at her, turning for the door. "Yes, that responsible," he waved. "Thank you all."

As quickly as they had entered they moved out of the room, and for the first time since the conference began, Greg noticed Joe Lannon was missing.

"Where's Mr. Lannon, Dad?"

The Senator stopped, nodding. "Here he comes now, son," his father said. "He slipped out of the press conference to look for a phone, to check on our plane."

They watched Lannon approach them with his face drawn with worry.

"What's wrong?" Hill asked.

"Trouble," Lannon answered, shaking his head. "Foul-up in the Transport Command. They may not have a plane till late tonight."

"That's ridiculous," Hill spat. "We'd be better off driving!"

"Eight hours?" Lannon questioned, shaking his head again. "No, I'll call Washington," he added, breaking off the conversation and moving off toward the phone again.

Senator Hill checked his watch and looked across

33

the concrete apron toward his Navion. He smiled pleasantly, placing a hand on Greg's shoulder. "Son," he said, "Joe has a habit of worrying unnecessarily. Let's get back to the Navion. Let's see what kind of charts we have in the old ship's cockpit."

CHAPTER FOUR

Steve Austin felt the sun on his face and enjoyed its warmth along with the fresh scent of a new day. He stood outside of the entrance to his motel, waiting for his ride to the airport, reviewing in his mind every detail of his simulator ride with Senator Hill.

The more he thought about it, the more he realized how many details and questions were yet to be explored. The crash had taken the lives of four crew members, among them a truly great pilot Steve had known for years. Tom Jeffers had been no slouch in anyone's cockpit. It was difficult for him to imagine Tom Jeffers not calling to Hill's attention that the number-four engine was out. Hell, if by some remote chance the engine failure did not show up on the instrument panel, why then didn't the flight engineer notify the pilot? And if by chance, no matter how remote, all instrumentation failed during their final approach, why didn't Hill sense the loss of power as he had sensed it in the simulator? A pilot with Hill's experience should have known something was wrong. If not Hill, then Jeffers.

Dammit, Austin, you're picking nits. You weren't there, he reprimanded himself. You are a reserve officer and the Air Force has called you to testify on cockpit procedure in the VC-135. Just do it—accurately and truthfully.

He forced his thoughts of the crash from his mind and glanced at his watch. His ride was late, and he moved his fingers along his jacket, checking to make sure his dress blues were properly buttoned. His awareness of his uniform with eagles on the shoulders caused him to grin. Not too often in the past two years had he played the role of Colonel Steve Austin. But his ordered appearance before the Board of Inquiry demanded it.

He glanced at his watch again. Perhaps he should—

A sudden blast of an automobile horn startled Steve, and he looked up to see a convertible coming into the motel's drive. Damn, he cursed softly, recognizing the man behind the wheel. Oscar Goldman from the Office of Special Operations, the man whose orders he'd followed on more secret missions in recent months than he cared to be reminded of at the moment.

"Hi." Goldman smiled, braking the convertible to a stop. "What a coincidence."

"Coincidence, hell," Steve barked. "Oscar, with you, nothing is a coincidence. What are you doing in San Diego?"

"Getting a suntan. You?"

"Well, I was waiting for an Air Force staff car," Steve frowned, "but I have a feeling you've replaced him."

"Could be," Goldman shrugged. "Get in. I'll drive you to the airport."

Steve Austin looked at the man behind the wheel with open distrust, hesitated for a moment, then threw his overnight bag into the convertible's back seat. He quietly climbed into the front seat, giving little notice to Goldman's smooth entry onto the street, beginning the drive to the airport.

Steve shifted his body for comfort, refusing to renew the conversation. He knew Goldman wasn't in San Diego for a suntan. The right arm of Jackson McKay, the director of the Office of Special Operations, didn't leave Washington without a reason. His time was too valuable.

36

Both men, Steve grinned to himself, were anything but what they seemed. This he'd learned only too well on assignments for them during the past two years.

His memories of Jackson McKay sitting immobile, like a hulking Buddha, behind his desk were most clear. A fat man with thirty years of intelligence and espionage work. An efficient killer with his hands or any weapon at his disposal. A veteran of British Intelligence and Interpol. One of the men who made up the hard core of the World War II Office of Strategic Services. From OSS to CIA, and then this new organization, OSO—Office of Special Operations; specialist *nonpareil* to all other security and intelligence organizations. McKay was one of the few men in the Washington intelligence hierarchy who was not soundly cursed by those he worked with.

And the man across the seat from him? Oscar Goldman? Hell, he wasn't in San Diego for any damn suntan. Not Oscar Goldman, Steve laughed under his breath. Not McKay's right hand, the fat Buddha's alter ego.

Steve almost broke his laughter aloud with the thought of how Goldman did not look his part any more than the corpulent McKay did his. Six feet of bones in a meatless frame weighing in at 149 pounds is a killer? The question brought a broad grin to his face, and Steve turned to stare at the passing roadside.

Dammit, he chided himself. He was being unfair in his appraisal of Oscar Goldman. He knew the man had served his apprenticeship as a special-agent paratrooper and ranger. He also knew Oscar Goldman was a genius in sizing up people, converting them to service for OSO. He was also a man with an extraordinary grasp of weapons technology. He had the truly rare ability to correlate an enormous range of facts from various disciplines. And his qualifications did not have a damn thing to do with the fact that Goldman could stand in the rain without getting wet.

When it came to getting the most out of people who worked for him, Steve Austin would be first in line to offer a testimonial to Oscar Goldman's talents. For Goldman, more than anyone else, was responsible for Steve Austin. Not *the* Astronaut Austin known to the world as the last man who walked on the moon. But Steve Austin, *cyborg*. Six million dollars' worth of biological engineering and electronics to put a shattered body back together again.

All the king's men couldn't get the job done for Humpty Dumpty, but Oscar Goldman sure's hell did it for him, for Steve Austin. And he—

"So, you're off to Luke Air Force Base," Oscar spoke finally, breaking their silence. "You look very sharp in your dress blues."

"Oscar, cut the small talk," Steve grinned. "You flew all the way here, so it must be important."

Oscar held his words for a moment before deciding to tell him why he'd come. "All right, it's important," he said. "I got a call last night."

"From?"

"From Joe Lannon," Oscar told him. "Senator Hill's administrative assistant."

"Oh." Steve looked at him. "Just a casual conversation?"

Goldman shifted his body behind the wheel and angled his shoulders the best he could to face Austin. "Not hardly," he answered flatly.

"Okay, Oscar, let's have it."

"Steve," he began slowly, "I'm very fond of Ed Hill. And I happen to know he's got a good shot at a Vice Presidential nomination next time around. That's *if*," he added with emphasis, "he's cleared by this Air Force Board. Now, your testimony will carry great weight with the Board."

Steve dropped his head to stare at his feet. "Oscar, I'm going to testify about cockpit procedure. That's all."

"But you know more!" Goldman insisted. "You flew the simulator yesterday. You crashed the plane the same way he did."

"It might have been the same." Steve shook his

head. "And again, Oscar, it might have been different."

"Fine," Goldman agreed. "So why not give Hill the benefit of the doubt?"

"Because if I'm not sure, I say so. I'm peculiar that way."

"Steve, I just want you to give the man a break—"

"Turn left, Oscar," Steve interrupted.

"What?"

"Turn left, or you'll miss the airport."

"Oh, awright," Goldman snapped, driving the convertible through the turn onto the airport road.

Both men held their words, and Goldman, disgusted because the trip was ending before they could settle the issue, maneuvered the convertible through the thick airport traffic. Moments later he was angling the car into a parking place near the Executive Aircraft Terminal.

Once parked, Steve got out and turned to face Goldman. "Well, thanks for the ride, Oscar," he smiled. "I'll try to forget the conversation."

Goldman hesitated while Steve slammed the door and lifted his overnight bag from the back seat.

"Austin, hold it right there," Oscar spoke in a commanding voice. "The conversation's not over yet."

Steve stood erect, eyeing the man who came nearer than anyone to being his direct *boss*.

"I asked you to give the man a break," Goldman continued. "I think you're entitled to know why."

"I'm listening."

"The fact is, Steve, I owe Ed Hill. And so do you."

"Go on."

"Two years ago McKay and I needed six million dollars. Ed Hill rammed that money through an appropriations committee, no questions asked, because he respected our need for secrecy. He still doesn't know what that six million dollars was for."

"I understand," Steve said quietly. "If it had not been for Senator Hill, there'd be no Steve Austin today." He shook his head. "But, Oscar, there's not too damn much I can do about it."

"The hell you say," Goldman said with heat, slapping a fist on the dash. "Just tell them about the simulator. The accident could have happened that way, right? Make them believe it."

"I can't, Oscar," Steve said sadly. "*I* don't believe it."

"Steve, that's not good enough!"

"It'll have to be, Oscar. I'm not going to lie about it."

"Dammit, Austin, you don't leave me any other choice," Goldman said flatly, gripping the wheel with both hands. "I'm not asking you, I'm telling you! Just do it, understand?"

"You're *telling* me, Oscar? You mean like an order?"

"Call it whatever you like," he said, no longer facing Steve. "Just do it!"

Steve sighed deeply, bending his bionics legs downward to place his bionics hand beneath the car.

"What are you doing?" Oscar questioned. "Look, if you would come off your high moral tone long enough, you'd realize that things get done differently in government and—"

Abruptly Goldman's words ceased. Suddenly the convertible was moving. Not forward. Not backward. But upward. He could feel the right side of the car being lifted, tilted toward him. "What are you doing, Austin?" he demanded with alarm.

Steve did not answer. The steel hand on his bionics arm gripped the beam in the car's frame beneath the right door. His bionics legs lifted the convertible slowly yet easily, an inhuman display of strength in a public place that alarmed Goldman even more. "Steve, stop it! That's an order," he snapped. But the car kept moving upward, slowly rising into the air. "Steve, dammit, put this car down!" Goldman barked again, looking about in panic to see if anyone was watching.

"Sorry, Oscar," Steve said pleasantly. "I don't like the tone of your voice."

40

"Aw, come on, Steve," he pleaded. "Please, put this damn thing down!"

"Why?" Steve asked innocently.

"Because, dammit," Goldman said frantically, "someone will see you!"

"Ah, really!" Steve smiled. "Then the secret will be out. The world will know. And I won't have to take orders from you any more, right?"

Goldman gripped the steering wheel in exasperation. "All right, you win," he said. *"Put me down!"*

The convertible settled gently back to the ground and Steve stood up to see Goldman sagging behind the wheel in defeat. "As I said, Oscar," he told him, still smiling, "I'll try to forget this conversation."

Goldman gritted his teeth as he watched Steve pick up his overnight bag and walk from the car. He studied Austin's smooth, sturdy strides across the flight line. He shook his head, his lips forming a grin. He was responsible for that! Today's Steve Austin. Half-man, half-machine that had just lifted his convertible with the ease of a child picking up his favorite toy. Not the Colonel Steve Austin known to the world as test pilot and commander of Apollo 17, the last manned flight to the moon, but the new Steve Austin. In fact, not an ordinary man at all. The Steve Austin the outside world knew nothing about.

Cyborg.

The Six-Million-Dollar Man.

A man Oscar Goldman knew was humanly vulnerable yet more than a man, an exquisite blending of shattered body, biological engineering, and electronics —a new cybernetic organism. A six-million-dollar man paid for by the United States Office of Special Operations. A man who had repaid his debt to the OSO tenfold by undertaking dangerous assignments, some of which had nearly taken his life.

The first had been an underwater expedition off the coast of Venezuela using android porpoises, during which Steve had worked his way deep into a Russian submarine cave and had nearly paid with his life for the pictures he'd brought out within his eye-socket camera. He'd been depth-charged, attacked by divers with knives, and shot. He had made it back with even *his* overwhelming strength nearly depleted and his bionics systems riddled and failing. Electronic "superman" or not, there were definite non-super, very human, limits.

No sooner had he been patched up than Oscar Goldman and the Office of Special Operations were pushing him back into action. They used Steve for assignments that were likely to be beyond most ordinary men. A brilliant mind and the build of an athlete combined with the bionics systems that made Steve Austin a cybernetics organism. *Cyborg.* Funny, the way they'd come to accept Steve in that role . . . he was so very human and vulnerable in so many respects.

There had been relatively conventional years as a test pilot, including three ejections from crippled, burning aircraft. Then came openings in the space program, and NASA had snapped up his application. Along with his experience and six thousand hours in the air went a master's degree in geology, another in aeronautical engineering, and still another in, of all things, history and cultural studies. After commanding the last Apollo mission to the moon, Steve turned down the Skylab program and came back to the sprawling flight-test center in the California desert.

The shuttle program was the program for the future. Nearly everything that would go into space, manned or robot, would make the trip aboard the delta-winged shuttle emerging from the drawing boards. There'd be a NASA shuttle and also an Air Force edition, and Steve Austin wanted in on the ground floor. The shuttle needed its principles tested in smaller forerunners known as lifting bodies, "flying bathtubs" to those on the projects. Wicked, given to sudden violent rolls to the right or the left, they were intended to breach the barrier reefs in the sky and get the flight and design problems solved so that the future shuttle could fly in comfort and safety.

Steve became chief project officer as well as chief test pilot with the M3F5. A B-52 dropped him at 45,000 feet. As he fell away, Steve ignited the rocket chambers in the belly of his flying bathtub. He took her up to 120,000 feet and sailed through a swooping curve from near-vacuum. As he began to bring her out of the high-speed glide she began her crazy rolling motion that was at the heart of the test—to find out what maneuvers by the pilot could damp the oscillations. He held her beautifully until he flared. He had it done, inches from touching down. She rolled, snapped to the left. Silver metal thundered across the desert in a flaming, disintegrating shambles.

Oscar Goldman had not been present that morning when the wicked little machine slammed into the hard, dry desert floor and ripped across the desert disintegrating, mangling a helpless Steve Austin. One moment superb test pilot, astronaut, human being of special talent and intelligence. The next, when the shattered wreckage ground to a stop in the desert, there was no man inside. Instead the rescue crews removed a battered, crushed, torn, and lacerated thing—mercifully unconscious. The rescue team was good, the medical team incredible—one doctor above all the others. Rudy Wells, bearded, moving through medicine and beyond; the only man who could venture, through his love and empathy, into the terror of Austin's mind.

The list ran through Goldman's thoughts: both legs amputated; the left arm mangled, torn from the body; ribs shattered, jaw smashed; replaced with metal alloys and plastics and ceramics. Beautiful open-heart surgery and implantation of a Hufnagel valve. There was more: blinded in his left eye; skull fracture; concussion.

The surgeons, especially two named Ashburn and Killian, kept the body alive. Rudy Wells attended to the mind and spirit of Steve Austin, subjecting himself willingly (because it was necessary) to Austin's abuse.

And Steve Austin survived. Precariously, but he survived. Wells kept him unconscious for weeks. Time was the friend now—time for the shock to dissipate from the system, for trillions of cells to re-form and to adjust to whatever life decreed for their intelligence of new inner creation. And then that was past.

The bionics laboratory was carved deep into the flanks of the Colorado Rockies. When the OSO learned what had happened to a man named Steve Austin, Oscar Goldman was immediately dispatched to the scene. The bionics laboratory was engineering and life sciences and cybernetics and biology wrapped up into a single gleaming package. There were men there who knew how to run through a giant computer every element of construction and movement of, for example, the human arm and hand. The computer digested what it learned, but so extraordinary was the creation of flesh and blood, sinew and tendon and muscle, veins and arteries and nerves, of bone and marrow and pulsing liquid flow, of trillions of cells, that the computer taxed even its own capabilities in reducing to intelligible numbers the handwork of God. The numbers finally were translated to digits with special meaning to eagerly waiting scientists and doctors and technicians. In those mathematical symbols they found the blueprints for creating a living simulation, fashioned from artificial materials, of what had been a human arm. Or leg, or elbow, or rib, or knee, or finger. It could all be reduced to digital form, and from that form could be re-created a living entity.

Some argued the semantics of "living." The human body functions on messages carried through electrical impulses generated by electrochemical reaction. Nervous energy is electrical energy, even if the wonderful intricacy of the human form seems to deserve a better analogy than to a weak self-powered battery.

Bionics did not contest the semantics. Nor did it solicit agreement. Their creed, under the direction of Dr. Michael Killian, was the work itself. Bionics. *Bios* from the Greek for life, and *ics* to represent in the manner after. A bionics limb was a recreation of a living member, and Steve Austin—cyborg—functioned

44

in a manner as unusual as the concept from which he emerged.

His heart valves were damaged? Replace them with the Hufnagel valve and supporting internal apparatus. His skull was crushed? Replace the bone with cesium and with new alloys where needed. Design a spongy center layer and another outer layer to protect the brain case inside. He could then endure a direct blow ten times greater—without suffering injury—than the sledgehammer thuds that had cracked his skull in the first place.

Replace ribs. Install—and install was the proper word—added tendons, plastic valves, arteries, and veins where needed.

Blinded in his left eye? Well, they weren't that good. Not at first. Not Dr. Killian, nor Dr. Wells, nor anyone else, because the human eye is a miracle of jelly and water and light-sensitive elements and rods and electrical impulses trickling their way through bundles of nerves to a gray convoluted mass of three pounds encased within the skull. So, they made use of the area where there had been an eyeball to build a marvelously small and efficient camera into where his living camera system had been. Steve Austin became a man with one living eye and one extraordinary camera that recorded on tiny supersensitive film what its human carrier saw with the living eye.

Later, when rapid-pace developments in microcircuitry allowed it, a tiny photomultiplier tube and zoom lens apparatus was built into a plastic eyeball and tied into Austin's optic nerve. It allowed him to regain stereoscopic vision and more: the multiplier increased the intensity of light by a factor of ten million when Steve willed it, and the zoom lens could increase the optical magnification by a factor of up to twenty. The photomultiplier tube, used most often to allow optical astronomers to push the capabilities of their instruments out nearly to the edge of the universe, now would allow Steve Austin not only to see, but to see in the dark.

None of this could compare with the miracle of the re-created living limbs—to the arm with its elbow and its bionics bones and cartilage and the never-believed dexterity of wrist and fingers and opposed digit, as well as the legs with their computer-directed systems.

It was one thing to construct the limbs that were to receive the nerve impulses flowing to and from the brain, nerve impulses that were electrical signals. It was another to mimic the nerve fibers and systems for transmitting the impulses from the brain into the spinal cord and on down the message networks. To Steve Austin's arm stump they double-engaged the bionics and the natural bone to exceed by far the original level of strength and resistance. They connected actual nerves and muscles and bionics nerves and muscles. But the signals that came through, while they well served natural flesh and its constituent elements, were hopelessly weak for a bionics system. So within the arm and the legs went small nuclear-powered generators that spun silently at speeds measured in thousands of revolutions per second.

The signal flashed through Steve Austin until it reached the part of him that was living by computer and machine lathe, where it was sensed and flashed to an amplifier. Now it was retransmitted at many times greater strength than when received. The small nuclear generators fed power through the artificial duplications of nature's pulleys and cables, which moved, twisted, pulled, bent, contracted, squeezed. But artificial fingertips tended to be insensitive, and a cybernetic hand could crush human bone with no more effort than was needed to pulp a rose. So they added vibrating pads, sensors, amplifiers, feedback. Now the steel-boned hand that could kill with a single transmitted impulse could also lovingly caress a lover's skin.

For months Steve Austin, reborn as cyborg, went through hell to create a physical and emotional knowledge and acceptance of himself. For months he stumbled and fell, weaved and swayed; his systems

46

jerked spasmodically, they shorted and surged; he was clumsy, crude, full of rage. But finally, with the devoted help of a giant of a man—in size and heart—by the name of Marty Schiller, a man with two artificial limbs, Steve Austin made it, and learned there were compensations.

If the bionics arm was not quite the same as the original limb, it was in many ways superior. The same for the legs. Steve Austin's arm was more than a human arm; it was also capable of performing as a battering ram, a vise, a bludgeon—a tool and a weapon. His legs were also tremendous pistons. His heart and circulatory systems served a body without the need of supporting two legs and an arm. The bionics systems with their nuclear amplifiers attended to all energy needs, and so Austin's endurance increased dramatically. He was dependent as ever on his heart and lungs and other systems. But he could run a day and a night because there was no energy drain from the legs hammering against the earth.

But what of the psychology of a man who had suffered impotence—not through genital injury or damage to the nerve network splicing the spinal column. No, through fear that no woman could feel or make love to a creature half-man and half-machine.

That, too, had been overcome; not scientifically, but by the oldest, most effective potion—the love of a good woman. Austin survived his crises, but he was still a man, and whatever superior powers he now enjoyed were still subject to the many ways he was vulnerable. A bullet through the heart would kill him. He could drown, suffocate, be poisoned, or be crushed.

His defenses did soar in efficiency, his reactions swifter than the most skilled athlete's. His body made him potentially a killing mechanism, especially when integrated with miniaturized weaponry in his bionics arm and legs.

Who else but Oscar Goldman knew the ex-fighter pilot's emotional as well as physical statistics? Six feet one inch tall, flat-bellied and wide-shouldered,

47

with a lean-muscled frame. An aura of confidence; blue eyes. Eye, the left one a miracle of plastic and microcircuitry, Goldman reminded himself. Those incredible bionic limbs . . . He would have weighed 180 pounds. He didn't. He weighed nearly 240 because of the metal and the other systems, but he carried it all with ease. No, not quite, thought Goldman. He carries it with the indifference of any man who knows what he is.

CHAPTER FIVE

Senator Ed Hill held the sectional air-route chart tightly, fighting a gust of wind to keep it spread evenly across the wing of the Navion. He rechecked the course he'd plotted and said flatly, "No sweat, it'll take us about two and a half hours to Luke."

Greg looked up, keeping his fingers firmly on the chart's border, helping his father hold it in place. "Joe's not going to like this at all, Dad."

"Joe Lannon doesn't run my life, son," he frowned. "We're going to take the Navion, and that's that."

"Whatever you say, Dad."

"You know what else, son?"

"What?"

"You're gonna fly right seat. You're going to be my copilot," he said with a comfortable smile. "I'll make a flyer out of you yet."

Greg looked away, across Lindbergh Field's long runways. "I don't know about that, Dad," he said thoughtfully. "I learned a long time ago not to compete with you."

"We're not competing," Hill protested. "It'll just be you and—"

"No, wait," Greg cut in. "You're so good at everything you do, I—"

"Is that why you chose pre-med?"

"Partly," Greg answered, his eyes fixed on the

49

chart. "Hell, son, you be what you wanta be, understand?"

"Yes, sir."

"Don't worry about competing with me, or following in my footsteps, or any of that nonsense, understand?"

"Right." Greg smiled.

"And I'll tell you what else."

"What?"

"We're gonna spend a lot more time together," he said honestly. "Get a few things done we've missed in the last few years, okay?"

"That'll be great, Dad." Greg's face beamed. "I know you've been busy, but—"

"Excuse me. General?"

Hill turned to see Steve Austin standing behind them, holding a salute. He let the chart go and stood erect to return the salute.

"Sorry to interrupt, General," Steve explained. "I was wondering what's happened to our plane."

"Doesn't look like we've got one," Hill told him, shaking his head. "Just thinking about taking my own ship," he continued, gesturing toward the Navion.

"It should get us there," Steve agreed.

"My son, Greg." Hill nodded. "Greg, this is Colonel Steve Austin."

"Steve Austin, the astronaut?"

"That's right." Hill smiled, managing to cover the strain that had developed between him and Steve the day before. "He's a witness at the hearing, too."

"Hey, it's great to meet you, Colonel," Greg said, extending his hand.

"My pleasure," Steve said, grasping the young man's hand with a smile.

"Hey, Dad." Greg turned to his father. "Here's the man to fly right seat with you!"

"Great idea, son," Hill acknowledged. "How 'bout it, Colonel?"

"Suits me." Steve nodded. "You're the only game in town."

50

Hill started to speak but held his words as the three of them turned to the sound of an Air Force jeep rushing toward them. Joe Lannon stared straight ahead, half-sitting, half-standing, holding onto the frame around the windshield. The airman driving braked the jeep to an abrupt stop before them, and Lannon jumped out, glancing momentarily at Steve. "Morning, Colonel," he said quickly, turning immediately to Senator Hill.

"Washington apologizes, Ed," he said before pausing to catch his breath. "They'll have a T-29 here in four hours."

"Well, eighty-six that," Hill said, gesturing toward his plane. "We've got a better way. We'll be there before they can get that plane here. We're taking the Navion."

"Now look, Ed," Lannon protested, "I don't think that's a very good idea."

"Oh, come on, Joe, don't argue," Hill ordered. "Get your bag while I file our flight plan. VFR," he added, "if that'll make you feel better."

"Fine, Senator," he spoke in a near whisper, conscious of the close attention Steve Austin was paying to their conversation. "May I see you for one moment?"

"Oh, all right, Joe," Hill agreed disgustedly, turning to his son. "Greg, help Colonel Austin with his bag."

"Sure, Dad." Greg moved to help Steve put his overnight bag in the Navion's baggage compartment.

With Austin occupied, Hill walked a short distance away with Lannon where he stopped and faced the man squarely, ready for the argument.

"Ed, this is really stupid. I don't want you to fly!"

"Dammit, Joe, you sound like a broken record," Hill spat. "Give me one good reason why I shouldn't?"

"You're taking a chance, Ed, that's why," Lannon answered, placing both of his hands on the senator's shoulders. "Let's get the hearing out of the way first. Your whole career's on the line!"

Hill stepped back from the man, twisting enough

to free his shoulders from Lannon's grasp. "Are *you* afraid to fly with me, Joe? Is that it?"

"That's not the question, Ed." Lannon tapped a finger on Hill's chest. "The question is, are you fit to fly?"

"Joe, let go of it," Hill told him firmly. "You've been like an old lady ever since the accident. Right now, you're convincing Austin that something's wrong."

"Ed, I—"

"Shut up, Joe," he snapped, his eyes dancing. "I don't wanta hear another word, understand?"

Lannon nodded, slowly.

"Now find your bag and get in that airplane," Hill ordered. "I'll be right back, soon as I file our flight plan."

The senator turned abruptly and walked toward the Terminal, not at all pleased with himself for having to be as blunt and firm as he'd been with Joe Lannon. After all, Joe had his best interests at heart. Had had ever since he'd first run for political office sixteen years before. But in spite of Lannon's value to him as a political aide, Hill knew the man must learn when to let up. When to let go. When to relax.

Hill shook his head and grinned. Hell, that just wasn't going to happen. Relaxing just wasn't Joe Lannon's style. In fact, without turning to look over his shoulder, Hill could see Lannon clearly in his mind—see how his aide stood, watching him walk toward the terminal, muscles taut and shoulders tensed. A troubled man, sweating, running fingers through a thick shock of white hair.

Regardless of Lannon's tenseness, over the years Hill had come to admire the man, to respect what lay behind the thickness of his white hair—a mind of shrewd perceptiveness.

Ever since the day Hill's wife Janice had brought Lannon into his political camp, there was no question in the senator's mind of just what his wife had brought into the organization. A man whose hunting ground was the political arena, a man who was skilled in cutting down those who stood in his way.

Joe Lannon was typical of his special breed. They were not immoral, because they had long since discarded morality. Fairness to them was a muddled concept of the very young or the very old. One purpose existed. Get what you need or what you want, and the righteousness of the act is determined by the results achieved.

If you fail, you're wrong.

And Joe Lannon didn't fail often. He moved through the shadows of the nation's capital like an ethereal lobbyist. He knew people and he had information people would rather not see released. Especially during the Watergate months.

Hill grinned again. Watergate had been Joe Lannon's finest hour, for there were at least a half-dozen senators and a half-dozen congressmen whose names would have been added to the public lists had not Lannon anticipated the government's blunders and moved swiftly to incinerate certain damning evidence with his characteristic speed and thoroughness.

Lannon accepted the inevitable welshers in politics, but they were more than compensated for by those who mixed their payments with gratitude. And this gratitude, Hill had often heard Lannon say, was a mistake. In political back rooms gratitude was an emotion that clouded a man's thinking.

On this point, Hill did not agree. It was just one of many areas where he found himself at odds with Lannon. For he knew just how much bigger and better a man feels when he allows himself to succumb to the emotion of gratitude. And Hill also knew, as he entered the Terminal with a smile, that every politician should have a Joe Lannon.

CHAPTER SIX

Senator Ed Hill cupped the microphone in his hand and cleared his throat. "Lindbergh Ground, this is Navion four-three-seven-two kilo. Taxi to takeoff. I have the numbers, over."

"*Seven-two kilo, Lindbergh Ground. Cleared to runway two-one.*"

"Roger, Lindbergh Ground, runway two-one," he acknowledged, placing the microphone back in its clamp below the instrument panel.

Hill made a final adjustment to his seat and looked about the cabin, briefly checking to be sure seat belts were secured and all aboard were ready for flight. Steve Austin sat quietly in the copilot seat, while in the rear Greg stared casually out the window and Hill noticed sweat beading on Joe Lannon's forehead.

The senator smiled to himself. Joe was born sweating, chewing his nails, he thought as he pushed the throttle forward, maneuvering the Navion among the rows of other planes. Moments later he was on the taxiway, moving toward the runway threshold. Once there, Hill stopped for a final check of the plane's controls and engine gauges.

It was a beautiful morning. Clean, blue sky flecked with bright puffy clouds. Great, Hill thought. What could possibly go wrong on a day like this? It'll even be hard for Joe to mess it up.

He completed his final preflight check and took the mike from its clamp, pressing the transmit button with his thumb. "Lindbergh Tower, Navion four-three-seven-two kilo ready for takeoff."

"Seven-two kilo, cleared for takeoff."

Hill turned to Steve Austin, gesturing toward the Navion's yoke before the copilot seat. "She's all yours, Colonel."

"No, thanks," Steve refused the offer. "I'm a little rusty on prop jobs."

"Come on, it's just like swimming," Hill insisted, "you never forget it."

"I'd rather watch you do your stuff, General."

"Okay, last chance to—"

"Seven-two kilo, are you rolling, sir?" the tower's irritated question came through the cabin speaker.

"Sorry, Lindbergh Tower," Hill apologized, "seven-two kilo, on our way."

The Navion rolled onto the end of the runway and Hill stood on the brakes, pushing the throttle forward until the engine screamed with power. He released the brakes and let her have her head. Thirteen hundred feet of used runway later the Navion eased into the air. Steve brought up the gear at Hill's sharp command. They had speed to spare by the time they crossed the escarpment at the end of the strip.

Hill reached for the mike. "Seven-two kilo, off the ground at one-niner. Will you open my VFR flight plan to Luke Air Force Base? Over."

"Roger, seven-two kilo. Flight plan activated at one-niner."

"Roger, Tower," Hill acknowledged, playing the Navion gently in a long slow climb out over the Pacific, passing the San Diego Naval Yard to their left. He waved his hand to attract the others' attention and pointed toward the ocean. An aircraft carrier came into view on the port side, its flight deck loaded with sleek jet fighters. The others nodded and moments later, Hill rolled out of his turning climb onto a heading of zero-seven-eight degrees and the Navion was back over land.

Hill keyed the mike. "Lindbergh Tower, this is seven-two kilo, clear of your area."

"Roger, seven-two kilo. Switch to San Diego Departure Control. Have a nice day, sir."

"Roger, same to you, sir," Hill told the tower, leaning forward to switch his VHF radio to Departure Control. "San Diego Departure, this is Navion four-three-seven-two kilo, over."

"Seven-two kilo, San Diego Departure, go ahead."

"San Diego Departure, this is seven-two kilo, outbound from Lindbergh on a heading of zero-seven-eight degrees, climbing to thirteen thousand five hundred feet, on VFR flight plan to Luke Air Force Base, over."

"Roger, seven-two kilo, this is Departure, we have you eleven miles southeast of Lindbergh. Report level at thirteen-five."

"Seven-two kilo, roger Departure," Hill acknowledged.

Next, he scanned the dials and gauges before him, cross-checking his instruments to make sure all were where they should be before beginning his survey of the air space around the Navion. Even though his aircraft was being monitored by San Diego Departure Control's radar, no experienced pilot ever left his or his passengers' safety to the absolute care of someone else in a heavy traffic area.

He completed his instrument cross-check and looked out, scanning first to the north, halting long enough to study the white beaches and rugged coastline they were leaving behind before moving his head slowly until he could see the Mexican city of Tijuana to the south. Satisfied the sky was empty, Hill returned his attention to the Navion's instrument panel. Airspeed, rate of climb, directional gyro, artificial horizon; all were in the groove. He watched the instruments carefully until he reached his assigned altitude, where he leveled the Navion off at thirteen thousand five hundred feet.

"San Diego Departure, seven-two kilo, level at thirteen-five," he reported to the control center.

"*Roger, Navion four-three-seven-two kilo, San Diego Departure. We have you twenty-one miles southeast of Lindbergh. We have no traffic in your area. Radar service terminated.*"

"Roger, Departure, have a nice day. Navion four-three-seven-two kilo, out," Hill signed off, cross-checking his instruments again. All was still perfect and he reached forward, placing the microphone back in its clamp before lowering the VHF radio's volume. Next he dialed the ADF (automatic direction finder) to a standard broadcast station's frequency. Then Hill settled back to enjoy music filling the cabin from the overhead speaker. The takeoff and climb to altitude and course had been silk. Time now to relax and enjoy.

In spite of all the hours he'd logged in the air, Hill never tired of the wonders of flight. He was very much at home and he gazed through the Navion's windshield at what lay before them. The music seemed to blend with the smooth air, and the San Bernardino Mountains hung on the distant horizon like a sawtoothed wall built by giants. From their viewpoint the mountains seemed slowly to drift toward the Navion, lifting gently but steadily. The altimeter needle was pegged at thirteen-five, and for the moment they enjoyed calm air. This was the time in flight when the sense of movement of the airplane seemed to be suspended completely. The Navion was a capsule sealed off from the rest of the world. The panorama of a mighty mountain range assumed a new dimension, and the men felt as if they were a tiny pod sitting there in the middle of a sea of air while the distant world came to them. Even the sounds were muted, the engine roar a distant murmuring. Human bodies had become attuned to the vibrations of the machine and, in harmony, no longer resisted such forces and paid little or no attention to them.

Hill turned his attention from the beauty before

them and looked over his shoulder. Even Joe Lannon was relaxed; he no longer sweated. The smooth flight had become a magic carpet even for him.

Hill turned back to study the panorama. Mountains of splendor were changing shape before their eyes, emerging from haze and slanted sunlight to become individuals in their own right. And then they were over the San Bernardinos, approaching across their southern range. At the same time they saw the sweep of clouds from the mountains' east slope, a thick layer of tumbling cumulous racing in to obscure the peaks.

They looked down, awed by the tumbled and jagged rock faces and peaks below them. The mountains were dark; rock that was black and dark brown, tinged with traces of deep red, and in the distance, with shades of gray-blue. Nothing seemed to live down there, not tree nor shrub nor bush. Just rock, naked and forbidding, with the only life clustered along its lower flanks, looking from their height like moss clinging desperately to its host.

The clouds had split the morning sunlight into huge beams poking down from the mists, magnificent pillars that seemed to glow from within. One huge shaft of light reflected brilliantly off water to the left of their flight path.

"Look at that!" Senator Hill pointed to the reflection. "See it, Greg? It's the Salton Sea."

"It's beautiful, Dad," Greg replied, twisting in his seat to tap Steve Austin on a shoulder. "But I bet it doesn't compare with what you saw on the moon, huh, Colonel Austin?"

"I guess not," Steve answered the young man. "But flight, any flight," he added quickly, "seems to always surprise you with its own special brand of beauty."

"That's a fact," Senator Hill nodded in agreement.

They turned their attention back to the Navion's windows. The San Bernardinos were fading from their view, and the landscape before them became a broad rolling plain. Hill reached for the ADF dial and lowered the music. "I'm gonna put her on autopilot," he

58

told Steve Austin. "Unless you want her for a while?"

"No, I think I'll get some shut-eye," Steve answered, loosening his seat belt. "Never could get any sleep the first night in a motel room."

Senator Hill nodded, switching on the autopilot to put the Navion under the control of automatic flight. He grasped the ADF dial again, turning the music level up, and loosened his own seat belt a notch. He was surprised to see how quickly Steve Austin was able to relax. The former astronaut had made the most out of the Navion's right seat; his body stretched for comfort while his head and arms seem to find just the right position to fill the space between the seat and door.

Well, why shouldn't the man be comfortable in that seat? Hell, Hill reminded himself, Steve Austin had not only logged his share of sleep in all types of aircraft, he was one of only twelve men to ever sleep on the moon. Not forgetting, of course, all the hours Austin had slept in the not-so-roomy Gemini and Apollo spacecraft.

Thinking about it, Hill shook his head. Sleeping in a tin can between worlds! it couldn't be all that easy. The Apollo sailing through space to distances a quarter of a million miles from its home planet! Good Lord, what a trip! He knew the great majority of pilots could never sleep on such a flight. Their eyes would be glued to monitoring their ship's systems, making sure the damn thing was going to get them back to that world they'd left so far behind.

Hill shifted his haunches. Speaking of monitoring instruments! He scanned the Navion's instrument panel. Everything was still in the groove, and he glanced over his shoulder. Austin's sleep was catching. He saw his son resting with closed eyes while Joe Lannon struggled to fall asleep. Hang in there, Joe, baby, he grinned, turning back to his window.

He watched the desert landscape slide beneath the Navion until he could see the runways of El Centro come into view. He turned to the right to see the border town of Mexicali; its streets and low buildings running east and west seemed to cling desperately to the line dividing the United States and Mexico.

Suddenly static and garbled voices fought the music to share the cabin's overhead speaker. Hill was instantly aware that the interference was from San Diego Departure Control and he reached forward, turning the volume down on his VHF receiver even more. Then he slowly turned the ADF's dial, searching for a stronger signal from a closer broadcast station. He found a program to suit his taste and once again pleasant music filled the Navion.

Nice, Hill thought. He enjoyed dreamy music. It reminded him of *that* problem he'd had months before. What was it that damn specialist had suspected? A possible astrocytoma of the temporal lobe? That's what he said it *could* be. A tumor. But he wasn't really sure. He had wanted to make tests, put him in the hospital for a few days. Damn, Hill cursed to himself. The reporters would have had a field day with that one. Well, he sure as hell wasn't going looking for trouble. As he'd always said, ignore anything long enough and it'll go away.

He laughed to himself. Dammit, he'd been right. It had gone away. He hadn't had any attacks for months now. Passed his last two Air Force flight physicals with no trouble at all. He was as normal as any man. His friendly flight surgeon had said so.

He leaned forward, turning the ADF dial. An instrumental version of "September Song," one of Hill's favorites, filled the speaker and he turned the music up even more. He hummed along with the recording. Everything was still in the groove. All was well and he looked through the windshield to see a familiar sight. High overhead, a jet painted its contrail from east to west. He's coming from where we're going, Hill mused, heading to where we've been.

The pilot of the Learjet never saw the small Navion three miles beneath him. He had more urgent things on his mind than sightseeing. "We should be in easy range of San Diego, now," he told his copilot. "Dial 'em in."

The Learjet copilot cranked in San Diego Approach Control's frequency. "San Diego Approach Control, Learjet three-zero-four tango inbound from Phoenix. I have an urgent pilot weather report, over."

"Learjet three-zero-four tango, San Diego Approach Control, go ahead."

"Roger, San Diego Approach, three-zero-four tango. The weather is going to pieces off toward Mexico west of Phoenix. Turbulence and massive thunderhead buildup. Thought you better let the boys know, over."

"Roger, three-zero-four tango, understand. We had one departure. We'll try to advise. San Diego Approach, out."

The flight controller turned quickly to his radar. "We've lost the Navion on the scope," he told the man at his side. "He's out of range."

"Radar range, maybe," the man said, "but not VHF."

"Right," the flight controller agreed, "I'll give it a try."

He keyed his mike. *"Navion four-three-seven-two kilo, San Diego Departure Control, over."*

Inside the Navion Senator Hill sat up suddenly, straining to hear what was interfering with the music.

"Navion four-three-seven-two kilo, I say again, this is San Diego Departure Control, over."

Hill reached forward, turned the music down and listened. Nothing but static and a faint, unreadable transmission. He shook his head, turned the VHF radio off and brought the music's volume up again. He turned to see Steve and the others sleeping soundly. No sweat, he thought, again relaxing, the music soothing.

"Navion four-three-seven-two kilo, I repeat. This is San Diego Departure Control. I have an urgent pilot advisory. Come in, please."

The two flight controllers waited. Nothing.

"*Navion four-three-seven-two kilo, this is San Diego Departure Control. I repeat. I repeat. I have an urgent pilot advisory. Come in, please. Come in, please.*"

Still nothing.

"Call Yuma and have them attempt contact when he enters their area," the flight controller told the other one. "I bet that idiot has his VHF off."

"If he does, and Yuma can't contact him," the man shook his head, "Mister seven-two kilo will get the message soon enough."

CHAPTER SEVEN

The autopilot moved the Navion smoothly through quiet air, holding to course and altitude as dictated. Nothing to do but observe and appreciate. It was that point in flight when most pilots permitted themselves time for thought. Time for the mind to wander. Senator Edwin J. Hill was no exception.

He looked about the Navion's cabin, paying little notice to the others sleeping about him. He was remembering the pleasant hours spent in *his* ship. And those yet to come.

Suddenly, there was no Board of Inquiry demanding his concern. Only comfortable memories. Times he held with far more affection than the notoriety he had achieved in recent years.

Somehow he could be certain of finding warmth in his memories of those chilly autumn days in Illinois when he would break away from the mainstream of clamoring students spilling from the classrooms of Lebanon High. He would rush off to nearby Lebert Field where he often rode his bike to the grass-strip airport just to stare at the planes. In the distance, he could see the Army Air Corps fighters and bombers claw into the sky from Scott Field. Sometimes he'd ride his bike to the road that crossed the end of the Scott runway and stand, gaping, as a fighter thundered over his head, tucking up its gear and fleeing like a mighty bird into puffy white clouds.

The great military aircraft awed him, but he'd soon return to Lebert Field and its short grass runways where he could get close to the planes. He would watch the pilots shouting "Contact!" to the mechanics, the wooden props swinging down suddenly and catching with a stuttering cough. He loved to stand behind the ships when the pilots revved them up for power checks. The air blast whipped back, throwing up dust, stinking of oil and gasoline. It flattened the grass, blew strong and heady into his face.

Soon, a young Ed Hill had become an airport fixture. He was the pilots' "go-fer." He gladly ran their errands and helped them with their planes, and he was fifteen when one offered him his first hop. The airplane was old, its fabric a faded and splotched yellow, and the engine dripped oil. It smelled of gasoline in flight, and it shook his teeth. But he didn't care. He loved the clanking, wheezing machine.

Afterwards, he offered his help even more eagerly, and the pilots made room in their craft. Most let him handle the stick and rudder pedals in flight, adding instructions when possible.

Then there was the day the man with the red-and-white Stearman biplane landed at Lebert Field. And young Ed Hill helped the pilot with the beautiful ship, running behind the right wing and pushing on the struts. They got the machine refueled, and he answered all the pilot's eager questions, bringing him coffee and a couple of fresh doughnuts. And while the pilot downed the coffee, Hill stood on a box, cleaning the cockpit glass, polishing the gleaming red-and-white surface here and there. The man watched in silence for a few moments.

"Hey, kid! Would you like a ride?"

The youngster's grin answered the pilot's question, and minutes later they were in the air where, for the first time, Hill experienced aerobatics.

It was an unforgettable introduction to that part of

flight where earth and sky vanished and reappeared with startling rapidity.

It began with Hill staring at a vertical horizon and realizing the edge of the world now stood on its end. But not for long, as the Stearman continued on over, rolling around the inside of an invisible barrel in the air, until the ground was up and the sky was down. He had just enough time to catch his breath when the nose went down and an invisible hand pushed him gently into his seat and glued him there as the nose came up, and up. The horizon disappeared again, and the engine screamed with the dive. Then the nose was coming up, higher and higher, and the engine began to protest the pull against it. The sun flashed in his eyes, and Hill found himself on his back as the Stearman soared up and over in a beautiful loop.

There was a lot more to it, and Hill's eyes were glazed with delight and wonder when the biplane whispered onto the grass at Lebert.

There could be no stopping him after that delirious flight. He lived and slept flying and drove his parents near distraction with his long absences from home.

He worked every afternoon when he left school. He saved, took a job on Saturday night, and spent his weekends at Lebert Field. There, he did odd jobs as well, accepting his pay in flight instructions; as little as a fifteen-minute hop made it worthwhile.

On his sixteenth birthday he had forty hours certified in his logbook, and the law said he was now of age to solo. That he did and almost flew home on his own private cloud. For there is only one first solo for any pilot, anywhere.

He graduated from high school in the summer of 1938 and went straight into flight school at Park's Metropolitan Air College in nearby East St. Louis, Illinois. He plunged into the world of flight with an exhilaration that ebbed slowly and only after he began to accumulate a growing number of hours at the controls. Exhilaration gave way to assurance.

The Japanese bombed Pearl Harbor the year he

turned twenty-one, and Hill volunteered as a flight cadet. At the time, his logbook showed just short of six hundred hours.

Within a year he pinned on his gold bars, but more important than being a member of the fresh crop of second lieutenants, he wore with a deep pride the silver wings of the Army Air Corps.

From there it was off to advanced training for fighter pilots. The biggest airplane he'd flown was the AT-6 advanced trainer, a rugged brute with six hundred horsepower behind the prop. At the fighter school he stood before the gleaming nose of a Mustang. He ran his hand hesitantly along one of the four big propeller blades. He spent hours with the sleek fighter, in love with its lines, burning with the desire to take it into the air.

He couldn't get enough of the Mustang. It howled with energy, and he took to mock dogfights with a fury, a fury he maintained in combat where, by the war's end, his Mustang's six heavy guns had downed four confirmed kills—one short of becoming an ace.

Following the war it never occurred to Captain Edwin J. Hill to leave the Air Force. He pursued the development of the new, high-speed jets with the same dedication and devotion he'd had for the sleek propeller craft.

When the Korean conflict broke out, Hill held the rank of major and was among the first group of fighter pilots to be outfitted with combat gear for the F-80 Shooting Stars. Flight after flight they pursued their targets in that lousy, cold place called Korea, and seventy missions and six kills later he was a jet ace commanding his own squadron—a group of the sweptwing F-86 Sabres.

Time after time he fought with the brass to stay in the air. They insisted his combat tour should be over. He insisted he was still one of the best damn jet jocks to sweep through MiG Alley.

Then it happened. At 40,000 feet over frozen earth. Hill was leading four Sabres when a pack of MiGs came sweeping down from high above the Yalu. They came out of the sun and they were on the Sabres before he could do a thing about it. There were twelve of them, and they scissored the Sabres, eight from above and four coming up from below to gut the F-86s through the belly.

Hill and his pilots took wild evasive action, breaking hard and swift to the right.

But at 40,000 feet the Sabre simply was no match for the MiG. The Russian fighter sliced its turns closer, it ran away from the F-86 in a climb, and it was faster. Hill watched big glowing coals sailing into the fuselage of one of the Sabres as the MiGs hammered away with their heavy cannon. Hill pulled his fighter around desperately to force off the enemy planes, but it didn't help. The Sabre under attack vanished in a great, angry, red splotch of fire. And the other two Sabres were nowhere to be seen.

He was . . . alone, in the midst of a hornet's nest.

He kept flicking away from the tracers. He abused his aircraft, but it was meant to be abused, and it obeyed him in the punishing skids and rolls.

He brought the fight to below 30,000 feet, where the Sabre came more into its own element, and here it was just as good as the lighter, agile MiG. In the bitter fight he caught two Russian fighters in front of his guns, and he watched the wing snap away from one and the pilot eject from the other.

The kills made him too eager, too anxious, and the reality turned him to ice when he realized that the two remaining MiGs had suckered him into a trap, closing from opposite sides at a moment when he had been climbing and his airspeed was low. They had him boxed, and he knew it.

Somewhere, deep in flight memories in the back of his mind, in that moment that demanded instant decision, Ed Hill recalled the narrow escape of another fighter pilot. He timed it with precision, waiting until the tracers flashed—until the MiG pilots were certain of their kill—and then his Sabre lurched and tumbled out of control. It flipped onto its back and whirled crazily. The centrifugal force in the cockpit dug at him cruelly, but he kept his hands off the controls. One of the MiGs followed him down to watch the sweptwing jet and its dead pilot. And suddenly the Sabre was alive, clawing around, and Hill watched with satisfaction as his six heavy guns streamed lead into the Russian fighter, exploding the MiG into a massive burst of fire before his eyes.

Back at the base, what Hill knew was confirmed. The three Sabres in his flight had been downed. He was the only one who returned.

Painfully, although the record did not indicate it, Hill accepted the responsibility for leading his flight into the MiG trap. No one agreed with him. No one in the Air Force pointed an accusing finger. But Hill knew it was time for another assignment. Time to go home.

Hill returned to the states with a new sense of commitment. The bloodletting of Korea had had an effect upon him he could not have anticipated. The eager fighter pilot, the hawk so swift of wing and temperament, had evolved. Hil was unaware that he had returned from Korea with a maturity which, had it been described to him, he would have vehemently denied.

He paused only to catch his breath and signed up at once for flight duty. But the Air Force told him to wait, to take a few weeks of leave until they could find a job befitting his rank and experience.

Hill went home, back to the quiet country that was southern Illinois. And no sooner than he'd traded Air Force chow for his mother's cooking, he was grateful for the respite from the grueling pace he had maintained for three years. He was content to spend his days in lazy relaxation. There was plenty of fishing, and mild surprise at the way girls now filled their tight dresses. It was a reminder that while he'd caressed sleek jets, Major Edwin J. Hill, at age thirty-three, had paid little notice to the opposite sex.

Oh, he'd dated his share of girls right enough, and, in high school, one girl in particular—Janice Carter, daughter of Congressman Andrew W. Carter.

Many years ago, before his Air Force career, Janice had been the girl he had dated regularly, and while neither of them ever had broached the subject directly, everyone assumed that marriage was in their future.

Well, the assumption had proved incorrect. Janice got married, all right. But to someone else while he was away. Now he'd been home less than a day when his mother volunteered the news that Janice was divorced, and was now *the* hostess of Lebanon. His mother stated flatly that he should call her. After two weeks of fishing and not much else, Hill did just that. He was pleased by Janice's unconcealed pleasure at hearing his voice. And, after a week of seeing her every night, he was pleased to find her, as she had been years before, uninhibitedly frank. At her suggestion they disappeared in a friend's cabin on the Mississippi for four days.

When they returned, Hill found a letter waiting for him. It was from the Air Force; he was to report to— he couldn't believe it—March Air Force Base. Assignment in Southern California. Sun, oranges, and movie stars. He was to command an all-new F-86D Sabre fighter group. And with the job went the rank of lieutenant colonel.

At first it didn't occur to him. But as weeks wore on and Lieutenant Colonel Ed Hill rolled his Sabre high above California's mountains and green valleys, he became aware of a certain emptiness. Flight alone no longer fulfilled him. There was, for the first time, another need. The companionship of a woman. A home! A family!

He sent for Janice, and she came eagerly. They were married and the first few months were spent pleasantly in the small house on Palmdale Lane in Riverside.

That's where Greg was born, a son to make any father's chest swell.

But the months became years, and Janice grew tired of the mother's role. She missed the campaigns and politics of her father's house. Soon she was wrapped up in local party matters and she was dragging him off to all manner of political functions. Hill found himself called on to make speeches and to his surprise, he wasn't too bad at it. Janice didn't miss this new-found talent of her husband's.

In time, Hill found he was promoted to the rank of full colonel. He often thought his eagles, as well as other accommodations in the Air Force to fit his new image, came with the compliments of U.S. Congressman Andrew W. Carter, who wasn't above leaning on the Pentagon.

It all seemed to follow a script, and Hill found himself not minding too much. In fact, he was rather enjoying the speeches and political maneuvers when Janice announced they were moving to San Diego.

"San Diego! Why?" he'd asked.

Because it was the largest city in a congressional district that was being vacated by retiring Congressman John S. Simmonds. And Colonel Edwin J. Hill had a good shot at it, and with the backing of—

What the hell, Hill thought. It's all history, now. He resigned from active duty, ran for the seat, and won. First it was smooth wine and rose petals. Then, as the years and congressional terms wore on, politics began to smell, leaving him with two sanctuaries— his son and the flights necessary to maintain his flight status.

This clinging to a part of the Air Force not only kept him in the air but legitimately advanced his rank, without too much outcry about political promotion, to brigadier general.

And if there had been any problems, there had always been Joe Lannon, image polisher and Mr. Fixit. Joe had been there from the start, in the first campaign in San Diego, through all the years, along with

Janice, insuring, pushing for him to run for the Senate. It hadn't been tough at all. Lannon's expertise put him in the Senate easily.

But politics really never fulfilled Ed Hill. It robbed him of the time to get to know his son. It robbed him of time in the air. And that damn specialist had talked about tumors, relapses, blackouts, telling him he was not to be trusted at the controls of aircraft. He should submit to tests. Take himself off flight status.

Well, to hell with him. He wasn't going to give up flying. Not Ed Hill. The left seat of his Navion was his own personal hideaway, and as soon as they reached Luke and that damn Board of Inquiry was behind them, well, he'd start living for Greg and himself.

Oh, they were talking about him as the next Vice Presidential nominee of his party. Well, the hell with "they." With Joe Lannon, with Janice, with—

He—

Suddenly the Navion was shredding small clouds with its passage, whipping through scattered rain, and Hill sat up alertly, the mind of a seasoned pilot shedding the thoughts of the past, instantly aware of the present. Before him were beads of moisture, driven by the wind, starting to drift around the windshield.

"Scattered clouds, they said," he cursed, shifting in his seat, abruptly aware of yet another problem.

As quickly as the Navion had flown into the gathering storm clouds, Hill sensed *the* feeling, the deadening of his nerve ends, the onslaught of one of the attacks he hadn't experienced for months.

For God's sake, not now, he cursed with a touch of panic, moving his eyes quickly over the instrument panel to see the dials blur before him. Dammit, no doubt about it. He was slipping away again. Much the same as those times before.

He looked about the cabin, realizing Steve and the others were still asleep. He twisted his head back and forth, wiping his forehead, trying to shake the feeling, suddenly aware of his aloneness.

He stared straight ahead, straining to see beyond

71

the thick and ominous clouds. More puzzled than alarmed, Hill reached for the throttle and added power. The Navion began to climb slowly.

For a moment he thought about waking Steve Austin. Instead, he reached for the microphone, but felt it slip from his hand. He reached forward, fighting blurred vision, and gathered the mike from the floor.

"Yuma Radio, this is Navion four-three-seven-two kilo," Hill said slowly, pausing to hear only static at a low level, mixed with distant music.

Christ, he snapped to himself. The ADF is up, and the VHF is down. He reached forward to kill the ADF volume and turned up his VHF. "Yuma Radio, this is Navion four-three-seven-two kilo," he managed to say.

"Navion seven-two kilo, Yuma Radio, we've been expecting you."

"Roger, Yuma Radio, I am . . ." Hill tried to force the words into the mike. "I'm almost twenty miles northwest . . . uh . . . VFR to Luke, and . . . I've got marginal weather . . ." He released the mike button and shook his head again, wiping the back of his hand across his eyes. He re-keyed the mike. "Is Luke still open?" he asked.

"Seven-two kilo, stand by."

Hill waited, blinking, rubbing his face with his free hand. He fought the feeling, realizing he was losing the battle. He tried to lift the microphone, only to have it drop from his hand into his lap. His eyes stared straight ahead, through the blur, his mouth open, a slight tremor shaking his head and upper torso. Once again he tried to lift his hands. He failed.

"Seven-two kilo, Yuma Radio. Luke is still VFR, but severe thunderstorm activity is developing along your route. Suggest you detour north and let us file an instrument flight plan for you through Albuquerque Center. Over."

Hill wanted to answer but he couldn't. He sat there, immobile, his breathing heavy and regular.

"Navion seven-two kilo, did you read?" the ques-

tion blared from the speaker. "*I say again, Navion seven-two kilo, Yuma Radio, did you read my last transmission?*"

Perspiration showed on Hill's face from a pale glow illuminating the cabin interior. Although he couldn't move or speak, he saw the lightning miles away. There were still open breaks in the soaring cloud mountains ahead. At the moment the storm wielded a magnificent and frightening paintbrush. The last traces of sun, the final gasp of a vanishing world, a golden hue preceding the onslaught of the storm.

But Hill did not see this. His eyes had become fixed on a single shaft of sunlight, a light swelling in size and in brilliance, washing away the darkness of the storm. It shone from within, and it brought him comfort, and he heard the distant, faint sounds, and he knew it must be music, it must be angels? and the sound rose and soared as the light rushed upon him, and he knew he was being received by—

The light wasn't shining.

It was burning.

A huge ball of fire, its flames shrieking now as it stopped before the Navion, fire hissing and crackling, a growing thunder, and there was no music, only a thousand, a million, a billion voices mocking him, shrill, tearing him into little pieces.

What do you want?

No answer. Only his body lifting gently from the seat, out of the Navion, floating upward, not knowing its substance, carried away by the billion throats in their shrieking laughter. The fire blazed and from its terrible brilliance appeared darker forms, *men in uniform, all general officers with stars on their shoulders, and he stared at their pointing fingers, and—*

The light vanished.

The fire was gone.

The universe stretched before him forever, and there were only the general officers seated at a long table, their angry words crashing through the darkness, their

73

shouts thundering in his brain, a staccato thunder-roll of fists smashing against the table.

He tried to go to them, to explain. But the harder he tried, the farther they moved away, ignoring, until they vanished into darkness.

He was alone.

Drifting in space.

An invisible hand grasped him, swept him away like a leaf in a high wind, hurled him into a dark hole swallowing him from all sides, and it was invisible and yet it was gleaming wetly, and he was falling into Eternity where the no-wind chilled his body and squeezed his heart and huge hands grasped him, cradled him gently and settled him on a long and beautiful pathway. Beyond the path, beyond his reach, phantom-like, Greg, smiling, and he cried with tears, but without them and—

The grass reached out about his ankles, beckoning him on. Life. It was there, all about him, the earth itself was alive and it flowed to him, and the trees were living creatures with green-golden-silver, swaying into a canopy through which there shone a glorious golden light.

That way, Ed Hill.
That's right.
Follow the path.

CHAPTER EIGHT

Arizona's Valley of the Sun is a strange world within a world, a monotony of flat, nearly sterile nothingness. Yet in the midst of this savage world, life struggles. Hugging the sand are sagebrush in coats of grayish green; looming upward are the uncaring and distorted forms of the Joshua trees. They are the giants of the desert land, giants thirty feet tall, defying all the odds of survival in the parched flatness bordered by mountains stretching from horizon to horizon.

Frequently the wind comes screaming down from the rock-strewn peaks, lashing the valley and blowing into the air enormous clouds of swirling dust and sand. Clumps of tumbleweed race ahead of the blinding sand like terrified animals fleeing a sea of fire. Sometimes their flight is arrested by the treacherous needles of the crooked cactus, and there ensues a grotesque scene of tumbleweed struggling desperately with the wind to escape before the roaring sand engulfs and devours it.

There are creatures of the sky that cast their shadows across the desert, over the concrete runways and structures that loom from Luke Air Force Base. Aircraft that send out shock waves, hurl thunderbolts through the skies to crash against the ground. They are the machines with razor-thin wings of the 58th Tactical Fighter Training Wing that slash the air faster than sound and hammer the world with the concussion shocks of supersonic booms. Luke is home to the largest fighter wing in the United States Air Force.

Standing high above the concrete runways is the glass tower from where the creatures of speed are launched and landed. Another room nearby is crammed with the latest electronics and radar to guide the swift jets through their flights. This is one of two such facilities called Ground Control Approach Radar. The other is located at Luke Auxiliary Field Number One. Either station can track the sleek jets while controlling with precision their return to earth.

One of those who manage this exacting machinery is Sergeant Jill Denby, a slender brunette of twenty-six who takes as much pride in personal grooming as in her ability as a flight controller. Those who know her are quick to testify she's no slouch in either, and, since reporting to the 2037th Communications Squadron at Luke, everyone found her fresh beauty as pleasing as her keenness on the job.

At the precise moment Navion 4372K flew into the building storm front, Sergeant Jill Denby was climbing the stairs to the flight control facility to begin her shift. She was in no hurry. She was early. It wasn't because of any enthusiasm she had for aircraft. It was the fear she felt for the safety of those who flew the sleek jets, a passion to assist them with all her skills, which had driven her to become the best possible flight controller.

On her way up the stairs she needed no reminder that deep inside her she hated the screaming jets. Such a machine had taken the one most dear to her. A sandy-haired, broad-shouldered creature with an infectious grin. The best running back ever to carry a football for Plant City High. A girl's dream; and he, Mark Wiggins, was all hers. But only for such a short while.

No, she had no love for flight. She never told Mark of her fear. Through his flight training, and when the Air Force parted them for Mark's tour in Vietnam, she only encouraged him to have faith in his abilities.

She stayed home while he was off at war, brooding that he would never return alive, that in a spasm of gunfire the body to which she had clung in their fierce ecstasies would be torn and slashed. In more than one nightmare, the thudding bullets ripped his smoothly muscled body from her arms and splashed his warm blood over her, and she tasted the salt against her lips and—

It was then she awoke, heart pounding madly, unaware that she had screamed his name.

She swore to herself that if the man she had loved since he was a boy should survive . . . that if Mark escaped the bullets destined for him, she would *always* be his.

Her dreams alternated between garish nightmare and physical longing. She realized one night, awakening suddenly, that her body had arched to meet his in deep embrace.

Now he was gone, and she knew that where he was, metal wings glittered in the high sun and young bodies jerked and shuddered from the tearing metal, and life vomited away in bright red chunks, and they were tearing his body from her arms and . . .

She came screaming out of the nightmares.

And then the telephone rang. The nightmare was real. A SAM missile had downed Mark's F-4 Phantom over North Vietnam.

Two days passed and there were no tears left. Only the hurt. She knew what she must do. She enlisted in the Air Force with the promise that she would be trained as a flight controller.

She left Plant City the day before Mark's body came home in a flag-draped box.

Six years passed; *Sergeant* Jill Denby is satisfied —not contented—satisfied that she is doing with her life the best she can to fill the void.

She is two thousand miles from the warm Gulf beaches of Florida, in a dry desert world that offers nothing to remind her of what might have been.

She reached the top of the stairs and stopped briefly to look through the window across the runway patterns before entering the room where she was met with the familiar radar scopes and speakers amplifying the words of pilots in their approaching aircraft.

Jill took off her hat and jacket, placed them on the rack near the door, and walked briskly to the radar console where Master Sergeant Wilbur Cole sat, slumping over the microphone.

"Eagle eight-niner romeo, Luke Approach Control," Cole spoke casually yet distinctly into the mike, "you are cleared for visual approach, runway three-two-zero. Contact tower now."

He released his pressure grip on the mike switch and turned to face Jill Denby, glancing at his watch. "You're early, Sergeant."

"Oh, am I?" Jill smiled, casually discarding any notice of her eagerness to report for duty.

"After the third day the thrill wears off," Cole laughed, pushing himself away from the console.

"This is only my second day." Jill grinned nervously. "Who can tell," she continued, "I might make it as a vet yet."

"There've been bigger miracles." Cole winked at her, returning the grin.

"I guess." Jill nodded agreement. "How's traffic?"

"No sweat," Cole said casually, standing up and stretching his arms high to fight off a yawn. "Just one target. Tower has 'im," he added, nodding toward the scope. "Should be an easy shift. Weather's so bad to the south everyone's avoiding the area."

"Let's hope so," she said, taking Cole's seat, where she immediately fixed her eyes on the scope.

The feel of the chair was familiar but not comfortable. It seemed everything in the Air Force was man-sized, and Jill Denby's one-hundred-eleven-pound frame fought for balance and ladylike poise. It was just one of many adjustments service women quickly grew used to. She discarded the thought from her mind. She

78

studied the sweep of the radar and was mildly surprised to see two blips illuminated on the scope.

She turned to Cole. "There're two targets, Sergeant," she told him. "One showing a 1200 code."

He completed donning his jacket and leaned over her chair.

"See?" Jill pointed.

"So?' he yawned indifferently. "He's squawking a VFR code."

"I wonder if he knows he's headed right into the storm front?"

"Probably just looking for a place to set down," Cole assured her.

"But he's flying south, right off the scope," she protested. "Nothing but badlands and mountains in that area."

Cole threw up his hands. "Listen," he said wearily, "you just handle military traffic and leave the Sunday flyers to the FAA. Okay, little mother?"

Jill nodded and watched Cole leave the room, pausing only long enough to snatch his hat from the rack. Well, maybe he can leave it to the FAA, she thought, but I can't. There are people out there.

She turned back to the radar in time to see the local target disappear from the scope, her assurance that the jet had touched down on the runway. She looked outside to see the Eagle racing down the concrete, drag chute out and brakes grabbing to kill speed. Now she was left with only one target—the VFR code moving farther south, deeper into trouble.

Perhaps it wasn't her concern, but Sergeant Jill Denby couldn't leave it at that. She reached for the phone, ran her finger quickly through the numbers, and waited for the ring on the other end.

"Base Operations, Airman Anderson speaking, sir."

"Anderson, this is Sergeant Denby over at GCA," she said hurriedly. "Is Major Phillips in, please?"

"Yes, Sergeant, hold on."

She waited, suddenly wondering if she was being too much of a worrywart. She might find the operations

79

officer less than receptive to her concern over the civilian aircraft, and she would be in for an old-fashioned chewing out that wouldn't help her superior's appraisal of her abilities as a flight controller. A woman's lot was tough enough in a man's world without any idiotic slipups. Perhaps Cole was—

"This is Major Phillips, Sergeant Denby. What seems to be your problem?"

"Well, sir . . . uh . . . perhaps I shouldn't have bothered you," she told the officer, finding her choice of words difficult. "But I have a 1200 code that's flying into the storm front south of us, and—"

"Civilian type, VFR?"

"Yes, sir, that's right," she assured him.

"Does he know where he's headed?"

"I don't know, sir, I—"

"Dammit, Sergeant," the Major snapped, "contact Albuquerque Center, see what they've got on him, check the situation out."

"Right, sir, I'll get right on it."

"You do that, Sergeant, and I'll be right over."

"Okay, sir."

"And, Denby!"

"Yes, sir?"

" You *should* have bothered me," he told her pleasantly. "That's what we're here for."

"Right, sir." She smiled with a deep breath. "Thank you, Major."

Jill replaced the phone and turned to the scope. The target was still there, moving south into bad weather. She reached for the phone again, checking a card before her for the number of Albuquerque Center.

CHAPTER NINE

Steve Austin fell toward the moon, alone in a lunar module built for two. He wondered about this, panicky at first, but soon his attention darted back and forth between thoughts of his aloneness and the stupendous view. Then, the wonderment short-lived, he fixed his eyes on what he saw through the landing craft's windows.

He was quick to discover that looking down from space onto the lifeless surface, the moon held up a mocking face. The blackness of craters imparted false depth to the circular shapes; most lunar craters, especially those of medium size and smaller, were in reality shallow, dish-shaped depressions, mere dents in a rugged and rippling surface.

Even where the great seas and plains from afar seemed level and smooth, change occurred with a steady pace. It was as if he was in a microscopic craft rushing toward the satiny skin of a beautiful woman; the closer he approached, the more glaring became the blemishes and faults concealed from the eye by distance. The apparently flat surfaces of the moon presented much the same changing view, until it became obvious that before him floated the victim of a brutal game of celestial target practice, the results of billions of years of meteoroids plunging into its airless surface.

He fell steadily toward the moon, and the light

playing on the cindered husk rippled with the shadowed interference of mountains and walled plains and craters. Earth was the distant, lesser world, and he found this difficult to accept.

A quarter of a million miles away the blue planet was a dazzling liquid globe suspended against velvet blackness. It commanded space, captured the center of the universe. For long moments he stared in awe at earth. At *home*. He—

"Apollo 17, Houston. Stand by. On my mark, thirty seconds until landing sequence start."

Austin tugged the cinches on his body harness, assuring taut restraint. His legs were spread slightly, booted feet evenly against the deck of the LM.

He glanced at the glowing numbers on the panel before him. "Not much longer," he spoke only to himself. "It's been a long time coming."

"Seventeen, Houston. Fifteen seconds."

He glanced at the empty lunar module pilot's position to his right, wondered again why no one was there, and shifted within his suit. He applied elbow pressure to the arm braces at his sides, preparing for the explosive transition he knew was coming. From weightlessness he would be rammed into the hammering deceleration prior to landing. Taking the sudden change while lying on a contour couch was one thing; standing up was another game to be played.

Steve held his breath for the final seconds before the descent rocket would be fired as the LM slid along a flat angle toward its computed target. The interior of the lunar module glowed with soft electroluminescent lighting from the front and side instrument panels. Directly before him, in the center console, flight instruments and display gauges stood out sharply, a contrast of light against light. Through the triangular windows he could see the mountainous lunar horizon, sawtoothed against the blackness that lay beyond.

"Ten seconds, Seventeen."

Austin glued his eyes to the glowing panels before

him. Range and azimuth numbers glowed, changed, kept changing.

"*Five seconds.*"

He was almost at the exact moment of firing. At that instant when the LM reached a point 192 miles from the landing target, when the lunar surface lay exactly 50,174 feet below, flame would spear along his direction of flight. Blazing thrust to kill his forward velocity, keep him sliding moonward. A long, flattened glide on wings of centrifugal force and howling fire.

The numbers flickered.

It happened almost before he realized the moment was at hand.

A tremendous blow struck the bottom of his feet. Flame lanced the lunar skies, sound clanged wildly through the cabin. Braced as he was, still he sagged downward, dragged by deceleration grinding through his body.

"Damn!"

Austin gasped, a mixture of severe pressure and excitement with the moment. He increased the weight on the grooved armrests and his face reflected a savage joy. He reveled in the pressure clamped upon his body. His powerful muscles answered the punishment, compensated for the deceleration. This was what he'd waited, struggled, trained, hoped for over a period of many years. This was vindication. The thunder of the descent engine was sweet music to his ears.

"Man, does this damn thing grab you or doesn't it?" he shouted aloud.

The flame stabbed ahead of him. Deceleration built up as the LM blasted away her weight with the fuel gushing into the combustion chamber.

No sound carried down to the moon. Not a whisper of the blazing rocket engine reached beyond the cabin. Inside the LM, thunder clanged and beat through the ship. Beyond the metal walls silence prevailed as it had done for billions of years.

"*Forty-two thousand, Seventeen!*"

"Roger, Houston, she's in the groove," Austin exulted. "I'm sailing right down the slot. She's a sweetheart, this baby!"

He repeated the altitude and velocity changes to Houston Mission Control as they flashed on the panel. Altitude changed slowly, distance swiftly in the arrowing descent. Speed fell off, a steady progression, a trade-off of kinetic energy for reduced velocity.

Lower, slower the LM moved, riding the mathematically precise rails of orbital mechanics.

Landing legs outspread for the feel of the lunar surface, the silver-and-gold machine knifed toward the gently rolling hills that lay directly to the east.

"Twenty-five thousand, Seventeen!"

"Roger, Houston."

The shadows stretched far across the lunar plains, lancing outward from mountains and high curving walls emblazoned with raw sunlight. Down he went, racing across the surface, descending more rapidly in a steepening arc, Austin snapping out velocity, height, distance to his target, angle of descent.

"Twenty thousand, Seventeen!"

"Got it."

"Fifteen thousand."

"Roger."

"Pitch steepening, Seventeen! You got the horizon clear?"

"Uh, no, hold one, Houston, ah—"

"What's the problem, Seventeen?"

"Can't see the horizon for the clouds, it's—"

"Seventeen, there are no clouds on the moon!"

"Right, Houston, uh, wait one—"

A searing bolt of lightning crashed across the sky, rippling away in a drum roll of thunder. The LM shuddered from the shock of rough air and Steve Austin instantly knew the feeling.

Turbulence?

Rough air?

Lightning on the moon?

Christ, it can't be. Not—

84

He sat straight up in his seat and shook his head. *A dream! Dammit, Austin, you were dreaming*, he cursed to himself, cupping his face in his hands to massage the flesh back to life.

His vision cleared, and he stared through the windshield. All about them now were clouds and fog and complete grayness. Rain squalls slashed at the Navion. *Hell, this is no damn dream*, he cursed again. *That weather out there is real.*

He turned abruptly to study Senator Hill in the left seat. All appeared normal. There was no evidence, or hint, that Ed Hill had been in his *own* dream world, leaving none on board aware they were flying into their current predicament.

Suddenly the Navion crashed into more turbulence. The left wing dipped sharply and for a long, sickening interval they hung nearly vertical, the airplane rattling through the sudden fall. Steve watched Hill let the Navion have her head; no use fighting that kind of whooping downdraft. He was immediately impressed with the way the Senator handled the controls, and he watched as Hill felt the controls begin to grab again and Steve saw the seasoned pilot bring in full right aileron, ready with the rudder, bringing back to almost its full stop the yoke in his left hand. The Navion shuddered and banged metal together and then they were out of it. Only occasional beams of light now pierced the clouds, and the weather thickened with new storm patterns.

Steve turned and looked over his shoulder into the startled faces of Greg Hill and Joe Lannon. The abrupt turbulence had all on board wide awake.

He turned back and slapped a palm across Hill's shoulder. "Nice recovery."

"Uh, thanks," Hill acknowledged, straining to find a hole in the cloud front ahead.

"How'd we get into this mess?" Steve asked.

"Yeah, Dad, isn't this weather dangerous?" Greg added to the question.

"No sweat," Hill answered them. "I can handle it."

"Why didn't you wake me?" Steve asked. "I could've helped with filing the IFR."

"What?"

"The instrument clearance," Steve said, puzzled. "You did file an instrument flight plan, didn't you?"

"Uh, no, not yet, ah—"

"Hell, Senator," Steve snapped. "We've lost VFR, you gotta get an instrument clearance."

"Yeah, right," Hill agreed. "Call Albuquerque Center, file an IFR plan, and ask for a radar steer to Luke."

Steve shot Hill a confused glance but he didn't have time to wonder about why the man had delayed changing flight plans. He reached for the mike. "What's our position?" he asked.

"I'm not sure," Hill answered, shaking his head. "Dammit, Colonel, check it out. Must I do everything?"

Hill's quick change of temperament prodded Steve to wonder even more about their present situation. But he dismissed his curiosity to concentrate on the problem at hand. First, he leaned forward, cross-checking the omni readings with the DME unit. The air was becoming more rough and with the increasing buffeting, Steve found it difficult when he went to the Phoenix sectional aeronautical chart to pinpoint their location.

"Damn, this can't be," he complained. "Something's crazy."

"What?" Hill demanded.

"No, it's all right, it checks out," Steve answered, shaking his head. "Senator, you're ninety miles south of course," he said flatly. "We better—"

Steve Austin never completed his sentence. At that instant a naked bolt of lightning tore the clouds before their eyes, grabbing the Navion and shuddering it in its savage claws. For that long instant of hell everything they saw was reversed as if their vision was that of a photo negative. Spots danced brilliantly before them and their small plane seemed to float on pure, eye-stabbing light. A split second later the thunderbolt raced away from the terrible lightning, hammering at the glass in the Navion's windows, and went crashing through the small ship like a thousand thunder-creatures exploding into every corner of their metal craft.

Silence, then. But only for a moment. A second searing bolt of lightning savaged through the clouds above to flash along the wings and fuselage of the Navion. The great hammer of energy tossed them from side to side, and Steve Austin was quickly alert to the smell of burning rubber. *Wiring!* It singed some cabling and wiring, he thought as the stroke seem to return. It pulsed; once, twice, a third time, and as it flickered with unholy force it raced away, fleeing madly into the thick, dark clouds.

"Jesus, Mary," Steve heard Joe Lannon scream. He turned to see the Senator's aide bury his head in his hands as the man fought to control a trembling body.

Steve moved quickly. He shifted back forward in his seat and checked the instrument chart for the Phoenix area frequency to the Albuquerque Air Traffic Control Center. He reached for the VHF radio, dialed the numbers, and reached for the—*where's the mike?* That blast must have jarred it loose. He searched the floor, picked up the microphone, and pressed the button. "Albuquerque Center, this is Navion four-three-seven-two kilo, do you read?"

What was that?

The mike had not keyed the transmitter. He was sure of it. As he spoke he could still sense, could hear the overhead speaker was receiving.

"Navion four-three-seven-two kilo calling Albuquerque Center, do you read?"

No response. Only static.

He worked his thumb up and down quickly, pressing the mike button down again and again in an effort to make contact. No luck.

He loosened his seat belt and managed, in spite of the buffeting by the rough air, to get his head beneath the panel. He could smell it. Burnt wiring. The Navion's transmitter was lifeless.

He regained an erect position and turned to Hill. "No use, Senator," he sighed. "The lightning got our transmitter."

"How could it?" Hill protested. "How could it without knocking out the receiver?" He gestured toward the speaker. "Hear that?"

"Yeah, I know, but it did," Steve insisted. "We can't transmit, and that's that," he told him flatly. "You'd better hang a one-eighty while there's still time."

Hill nodded agreement with a frown as he rolled the yoke to the left and brought in rudder.

The Navion turned through the menacing clouds, fighting heavy turbulence as they all stared in shock. All about them, in every direction, towered black clouds. The storm had sucked them in, enveloping their small plane within tumultuous lightning and thunderbolts.

"My God, it's moved in behind us," Hill said, continuing his turn to roll out on their original course. "We'll have to go through it," he added, soberly. "Hang on, it's gonna get a lot rougher."

"No choice but," Steve agreed as they braced themselves for what unquestionably lay ahead.

The Navion charged into the heart of the storm, its passengers certain they were alone in a fight for survival. But at her console in Luke Ground Control Approach Radar, Sergeant Jill Denby sat watching the tiny plane disappear from the scope as she waited for Major Phillips to arrive with what she hoped would be instructions in which, somehow, she could aid those on board the small aircraft.

Between her location and where the Navion disappeared into the storm, another target moved across the radar scope toward Luke's runways. She waited, listened, then heard the familiar click of the pilot keying his transmitter to her speakers.

"*Luke Approach Control, this is Air Force one-seven-five, eight-zero miles DME south at angels two-five. Estimate Luke at one-zero.*"

"Roger, Air Force one-seven-five, we have you sequenced," she told the pilot, pausing before re-keying her mike. "One-seven-five, we have an unreported light aircraft west of your location, VFR. Do you show anything on your radar?"

"*Negative, Luke Approach. We're reading a standard thirty-degree weather and ground scan of our inbound track. Want us to make a three-sixty to the left and scan the area?*"

"It could help, one-seven-five."

"*Wait one, Luke Approach. We'll have a look.*"

Jill Denby waited, staring at the scope. Only one target. The Air Force jet inbound. The small plane was no longer visible. Not a trace. And there'd been no call from it to Albuquerque Center. But they were checking. Someone must know who—

"*Luke Approach, this is one-seven-five.*"

"Go, one-seven-five."

"*Still no joy on that VFR target, Luke Approach. If he's west of us he'd better get out his prayer book. That's one mean storm off toward the Growler Mountains.*"

CHAPTER TEN

Before Navion 4372K was a roaring genie of blackness with bristling tongues of savage lightning, with invisible sledgehammers of wind, waiting to suck the small plane into its maw and then close its giant, grinding molars on the Navion's fragile aluminum.

Everywhere those on board looked they saw the towering mass of the storm, and they readied themselves for the moment when they would be even deeper within its fury.

Senator Ed Hill gripped the controls tightly as the storm began its methodical grinding of his aircraft.

Steve Austin studied his chart of the terrain he could not see below, making mental notes of mountain heights while searching the map for the best possible place for an emergency landing.

In the back, although he tried desperately not to show his tenseness, Greg gripped the seat tightly. Joe Lannon openly fought off panic.

"Can't you slow it down?" Lannon pleaded.

"I'm right at maneuvering speed now," Hill shouted, pointing to the posted limits on the panel.

Lannon took a deep breath and nodded. Lightning exploded at them from an unseen place. It was a sudden flash that quickly vanished, and where they had seen the heart of the storm, they were suddenly there, immersed in black wetness, and the visible world became only the interior of the Navion. Now there was no question of the violence through which they tossed and tumbled, the aircraft's wings twisting in turbulence, the mixed updrafts and sudden down-smashing blows of air making a mockery of control.

The airspeed needle swung crazily from left to right, at one moment showing them in almost a full stall, the next instant a velocity great enough to bend metal. The climb rate swung from one stop to the other—a good thing it was indicating rate instead of actual climb or the wings would soon separate, the tail would be ripped away. Even the altimeter needle slipped across the edge of the normal world. Its indication most reflected the actual events. Flung aloft on a howling stream of air, they shot from 13,500 to 15,000 feet, everyone jammed by the violence into his seat. Of a sudden they hurtled in the other direction, plunging toward the rocks and ridges they knew were below. Up was more acceptable. The storm could throw you just so high and no more. It might spit the entire machine from one of its flanks, but beyond that was safety and smooth flight. Down was another matter. It could be lethal. They shot skyward then, a long moment of false calm, suspended, wings stripped naked of their lift. Just suspended between the forces of the storm; far below, to the sides and above, the ghostly orange-yellow lightning. They knew. Despite Hill's skill with the controls and their prayers and curses, they had to go down.

Their heads went tight with the sudden negative pressure. Lap belts dug into flesh as they heaved upward from their seats. Instrument readings sagged or went to zero in the sudden negative gravity. Nose down, wings heeled over, the sickening plunge began as they rode an invisible monstrous falling river of air. All about them, ghostly radiance, slight fingers of blue-white spitting from the propeller, from the nose, the wingtips, glowing about beneath the wings. Static electricity. St. Elmo's fire. They were supercharged with electrical forces unable to discharge. They fell, helpless, and they all knew fear. They watched the altimeter unwind, the rate-of-descent warning to which they could not respond. A long moment to stare at the water-filled sky and think of their drop toward the mountains. They braced themselves for the shock when they broke free of the enormous downdraft.

It came. The Navion's wings grabbed air and Senator Hill felt the plane respond abruptly to his commands. He flew the small ship in spite of the storm and every minute became an hour of muscles knotting within arms and legs, in the packed ridges at the sides of the back, in the neck and under the legs just behind the knees. Hill's fingers cramped; his forearms tensed until they felt brittle.

Several times Hill thought he'd lost it as the Navion fought its way from one violent blow to the next, never for an instant free of the forces attacking its surface. The storm was taking on a malevolence of intent; it was an enemy uproarious in its power, to be survived only by skill and endurance, by guile, by hope.

Blazing streaks revealed the monster through which they pounded. The sharp and acrid smell of lightning came to them through wind and rain, through the metal and glass of their machine. Searing bolts leaped from within clouds through the air. They smashed into the earth and others crashed upward from the boiling storm to disappear miles over their heads. Lightning dazzling white, yellow, sometimes orange from distance and mist, sometimes so white it became blue. Bolt after bolt, energy rampant through which they must prevail. Over the racketing clamor of their own engine, they heard the terrible, crackling thunder.

Ed Hill wasn't at all convinced they'd make it. It was all too overwhelming. But there was nothing else to do but to fly. He flew, fighting his machine with muscle and skill and instinct.

The Navion pitched and rolled, sliding awkwardly from one side to the other, the nose slewing around dangerously. Downdrafts were trying to drag them into the mountains below. The engine screamed, the prop trying to overcome the hysterical yawing and pitching motions forced upon the small plane by the storm. Repeatedly the Navion disappeared into mist or plunged through cataracts heaving downward from the sky, rolling and pitching in the darkness of the storm, then the world was instantly ghost white with a negative smear of vision as lightning ripped at them.

Then it happened. A thin line of black appeared across the windshield, fighting for recognition in the drenching storm.

"Oil!" Hill shouted. "We've snapped an oil line!"

Steve Austin brushed the map chart to the side and gestured, "Throttle back!"

"But I'm at maneuvering speed, I—"

"Never mind," Steve insisted, "just keep her above stall."

"Right," Hill suddenly agreed. "It looks like it could be coming from inside the cabin," he added quickly. "Colonel Austin, could you work your way under the panel and check the line to the pressure gauge?"

"Sure," Steve said, unhooking his seat belt.

He worked his way beneath the instrument panel, struggling to steady his body within the storm-tossed craft. He managed to wedge his shoulders beneath the panel structure, bracing himself with his bionics legs. Finally he was stable, his body a part of the erratic movements of the Navion.

He studied the maze of cabling from the instrument panel to the fire wall, quickly spotting a small crack in the oil gauge line. "Do we have a first aid kit on board?" he called.

"Yes, sir, Colonel, I have one," Greg answered.

"Pass me down the adhesive tape," Steve shouted, "I've found the oil leak."

Moments later he was binding the cracked line when the Navion plowed into another mighty updraft. The small ship was slammed hard by the hammering stream of air and Steve Austin got only the briefest of glances at a rupturing niagara of hot oil spewing toward his face. The pain sliced knife-like into his one eye.

Austin gasped with agony.

"Greg! Help him!" Hill shouted, not daring to let go of the controls.

"No . . . never mind," Steve called, reaching for his handkerchief. "I—I think I can handle it."

With his natural hand he blotted steaming oil from his face, his bionics hand smothering the hot spray from the rupture. The others couldn't see what he was doing. They would have been stunned at Austin's ability to withstand pain. But there was none. The sensors in his bionics arm relayed only touch and pressure to his brain, not pain. He wrapped the tape tightly around the ruptured line.

Before he was done with it, he'd used all the adhesive. He could still feel oil dripping through the tape. But there was no longer a gusher, and he emerged slowly from beneath the panel to fasten his seat belt.

He sat back, holding the handkerchief to his face. "Most of it is stopped," he told Hill, "but my repair job won't last," he added quickly, blotting the oil from around his eye.

"Colonel Austin," Greg said, leaning forward from the back seat, "let me take a look at—"

"I'm all right, Greg," Steve insisted, waving the young man off. "Help your father."

Flight had degenerated into nightmare, and Ed Hill had no time to concern himself with an injured co-pilot. All on board depended on him more than ever as he fought, in spite of the slow drain of oil from the Navion's engine, to keep the small ship under a semblance of control.

He cursed the hammering wind, the eye-tearing lightning. The meteorologists had promised scattered clouds. And Hill could not help wondering if those who drew up the weather charts ever put their own predictions to the acid tests. It was easy enough to be pontifical when you stayed on the ground and watched someone else disappear over the horizon into God knew what. Like this soul-tearing plunge from which they, even his son Greg, might never emerge.

Hill's thoughts kept returning to that final act they might be playing. Through all his remembered life he'd been a pilot with flying his desire and his fulfillment. Not politics, God knew. Not the Senate. Not even the White House. He was fifty-four years old and never realized how years were passing until someone or something brought the matter of age to his attention. Life had been a heady challenge of accepting whatever flight threw at him. It wasn't any different now as he fought the controls, soaked to the skin, his muscles aching knots bunched along his skin. He was virtually lashed into the Navion, his feet muscle-strained and quivering on the rudder pedals. Quivering from fear as well as strained sinew, fear not only of the battle of the moment but fear of what had been going on in his head. Of what happened during the crash, of what happened only a short while ago when he slipped into that familiar blackness to emerge trapped in the storm. Perhaps the specialist had been right. Perhaps he should have listened. If he had, he wouldn't be here now. With a national hero, his face scalded by hot oil. With a son depending on his skills and abilities to get them down safely. With a devoted aide. Hell, yes, he was afraid. Christ, that's what it was all about. You gotta live with it. Only he had had a choice, and now it was much too close for comfort as his muscles made his feet dance on the pedals and his knuckles showed white as he gripped and fought the yoke to ride the ailerons and elevators in the twisting fight for survival. The sweat ran down Hill's face and into his eyes, half-blinding him, but not for a moment could he relinquish his death grip on the controls.

Under the cabin lights and the stabbing glare of lightning, Greg in the back seat looked at his father, his face pale and drawn. Whenever the moment allowed, he strained against the seat belt to wipe the perspiration from his father's eyes, to give him whatever small surcease there was. Greg was frightened, but he fought fear within himself. There was a fatalistic attitude that came to a youth's aid in moments like these. You knew you couldn't survive. No one could; no machine could take this punishment forever. Yet you struggled and put faith in the man at the controls. If you were going to die, if it had to happen, then that's all there was to it.

He moved his handkerchief across his father's face, quickly, withdrawing his hand so as not to interfere with his father's vision. He looked out at the storm, then at Steve Austin nursing his blistered face, their world lurching madly from the constant violence of the Navion's motions. The storm permitted him a brief glimpse of the rocky landscape beneath them and Greg knew if it came it would be swift. There would be time for one last shudder of his heart. Only that and no more.

Lightning slashed a jagged streak far to their left just as Ed Hill managed a glance over his shoulder. He saw Greg's face silhouetted cameo-like against the corneal afterglow of the lightning. In that instant he saw his son's eyes wide, the dilation of his nostrils from the hovering presence of death.

He didn't need or want to see more. He turned back to the controls, to the erratic instruments within the panel, and stared at the oil pressure gauge. "Don't look—" A pause that made the others hold their breath. "Don't look good, Colonel," Hill said finally.

"What's the score?" Steve snapped the question.

"Oil pressure." They knew the rest before they heard his words. "It's starting into the red. We're losing it too damn fast."

"We've got two chances." Steve's voice came to them in a hoarse whisper, but his words got through the storm's roar. "Slim and none."

"Yeah, dammit, you're right," Hill agreed. "I've gotta put her down."

"And right now," Steve said flatly. "You're not

only losing oil, Senator, you've got a mountain range ahead."

"The Mohawks?"

"No." Steve shook his head. "We should be over them by now. It's the Growlers."

"Whatta you suggest, Colonel?"

"Hang a right to about one-three-five, try for the desert before we reach the Growler range," Steve answered him. "We may get a break in the weather there."

Hill nodded and throttled back, easing forward on the yoke to drop the Navion's nose. He glanced at the erratic altimeter. Still more than enough height to clear any mountains in the area, he reassured himself as the plane shuddered badly, not only from the tearing forces of the storm, but from its own engine. The oil leak was increasing steadily.

He dropped the nose even more to pick up speed and eased off a bit more on the throttle. Any reduction in RPMs would save oil, and even a few seconds could make a tremendous difference. He knew he must land while he still had power. That would give him the chance to dodge anything unexpected, even if the damn weather followed him all the way to the ground. He could maneuver with power; otherwise they'd be dropping down with a glider on his hands that—

"Hey, Dad!" Greg shouted. "Look! Over there! There's a break in the clouds!"

Hill's eyes followed his son's pointing finger. "We're not home free just yet," he told them. "Make sure your belts are as tight as you can stand it."

He rolled the yoke to the right, brought in rudder, and in spite of the storm's violence pushed the Navion for the break in the boiling clouds. He could sense gaining speed as they descended toward the window in the storm, and he reduced power even more, straining to see through the oil-streaked windshield.

Suddenly, in the distance, he could see a horizon with blue sky above, rock-strewn landscape below. He held the Navion in a shallow descent through the buffeting of the storm, paying little notice to the cheering from Greg and Joe Lannon in the back. It was as if they had all been awakened from a nightmare to find themselves warm and safe beneath the covers in their own beds.

He smiled as bright sun leaped at them through the opening in the storm. He rejoiced only for a moment before his concentration turned to the rugged terrain sweeping toward them. Now he had to act. He added throttle and leveled the Navion as the small plane shook itself free from the storm's violence. Now they had smooth air and gentle updrafts above the foothills bordering the desert.

He flew around a wall of cliff-faced mountains into a long, deep valley running north and south. Before him was level earth, more than enough to land.

"Stand by!" he shouted as he unlatched the canopy and slid it back. "We're gonna land!"

Greg loosened his seat belt and wedged his body between the two forward seats. "I've got the gear, Dad!"

"Right, son," Hill acknowledged, leaning out, his face in the blast of air. He had to see around the oil-smeared windshield.

The wind blast watered his eyes and he squinted against the pressure. Directly ahead he saw a dry river bed. He knew what they were like. Seemingly smooth, but rough with grooves and dips and brush and rocks. Still, it was the best they had, their only chance, because to the left was a high canyon wall and to his right were grotesque formations carved from the hard desert floor. At least that damn turbulence was behind them. Below was very little sand, a dry, hard-baked surface; it could help.

"Flaps down, son," he snapped. He would try and drag her in with the last remaining power from the engine.

"Okay, Dad!"

"Gear down, Greg!"

"Flaps down! Gear coming!"

"Right, son," he nodded. "Get back in your seat," he ordered. "Hang on, everybody!"

It looked good. He held the nose off and saw the ground rushing by through his left peripheral vision. The nose was high; he wanted full lift and drag at the same time, playing one against the other with the throttle, a delicate balance of wings rocking gently. He braced himself as the wheels scraped brush and rock and the propeller knifed into something hard, jerking the Navion with a thrumming cry.

"Damn!" he shouted, reaching to kill the engine, and he had just enough time to see the propeller come to a complete stop before the nose wheel slammed down and they were on the desert floor, the world a blur, their bodies hammered as the plane shot across ground, brush, and rocks. Instinct kept his feet slamming against the rudder pedals until the Navion came to a stop a few feet before slamming into huge rocks that reached out from the canyon wall.

They sat quietly, grateful, as they watched dust settle around the aircraft. Only minutes before, they were being tossed and hurled through a torrential downpour. Now they were safe on dry earth, and Senator Ed Hill stared at their only casualty—a bent propeller. *Damn,* he cursed silently. *Why didn't I kill the engine sooner?* He had no answer to his question, but he did have a promise to himself. This was it. He had no choice. The specialist was right. He was *not* fit to fly.

He unfastened his seat belt and turned to the others. "Well," he began slowly, "God only knows where we are. But we're alive."

"You were just great, Dad," Greg said, touching him lightly on the shoulders.

"Thanks, son," he answered, "but I should have never gotten us in—"

"Save it, Ed," Lannon broke in, gesturing toward Steve Austin as he placed a hand over his mouth.

"Oh, all right, Joe," Hill nodded, turning to Steve. "You all right, Colonel?"

Steve dabbed at his face with his handkerchief. "Oh,

I'm peachy, Senator, just peachy," he answered. "Except I've got this one little problem."

"What's that?"

"I can't see."

CHAPTER ELEVEN

Senator Ed Hill stood by the Navion's left wing, staring northward to the mountain range holding back the line of thunderstorms separating them from their present location and Luke Air Force Base. Just *where* they were was a mystery he had to solve.

He stood on dry desert under a broiling sun, wiping his brow. He laughed inwardly. They'd spent a good part of the morning fighting their way through the damndest thunder-bumpers he'd ever seen in all his years of flying, and now he was standing on earth which you'd swear rain had never touched.

He shook his head and ran a finger along the aeronautical chart, beginning his survey again. Directly east of them light stabbed through crevices in the dark sky, sending glowing shafts across the vast desert floor. Clumps of scattered tumbleweed took the form of soft puffballs among the rocks. Along the nearby canyon wall, midget desert flowers shone in purple and yellow. The sagebrush seemed to glow, but above all there rose from the flat earth the oldest denizens of this desert-nowhere, the great cactuses known as Joshua trees. Some of these grotesquely crooked giants reared fully thirty feet above the desert, frozen in some ancient torment, and it was difficult for Ed Hill to realize these cactuses had stood here as long as the towering redwoods rooted in the great north-west.

He returned his attention to the chart. They had landed in a dry river bed. Just *which* dry river bed he now must determine.

He looked to the northeast. In the distance rose a towering mountain range. Those peaks had to be the Growlers. He moved his eyes left to more mountains bordering the desert to the northwest; they must be the Mohawks.

His finger moved along the chart again, following a dry river bed that meandered southward into the Cabeza Prieta National Wildlife Refuge. "That's it! We're here," he said aloud. "On the northern edge of the wildlife refuge."

He scanned the chart for towns surrounding their newly discovered location. There were none. "Damn," he swore softly. "Nothing for miles."

He searched the map, and his finger stopped on the town nearest them, the small village of Ajo to the east. He quickly computed the mileage. "Good God!" he swore again. "Twenty miles, at least."

Disgusted, he folded the chart and climbed the wing to place it back in the cabin. No way of walking out of this Godforsaken place. Not in this damn heat. Not without water.

He wiped his brow and stepped back to the ground. The only thing to do was wait and hope. Hope Air Rescue could find them before thirst—

He turned quickly, his thoughts interrupted by the approach of Joe Lannon.

"Hell, Ed," his aide said, wiping his brow. "Some of that rain we just flew through would feel great along about now."

"I'll take the heat, Joe," he replied, smiling.

"I don't suppose we have a choice." Lannon frowned, studying Hill. "What are our chances, Ed?"

"Desert heat and no water? The nearest town at least twenty miles away. What do you think, Joe?"

Lannon spat in the desert dust. "Well, I don't suppose it really matters," he snorted. "You've blown it anyway."

Hill stared at his aide but held his silence. He knew Joe Lannon, knew he'd just begun to complain.

"Sixteen years I've worked, Janice has worked to get you to the top, and you blow it because you can't keep your hands off—off airplanes," Lannon moaned. "I mean, women, hell, Ed, that I could understand, but—"

"That's enough, Joe," Hill snapped. "I realize more than you what I've done." He turned from the man to stare across the desert. "Besides," he continued, "we're not dead yet. A crash landing isn't the end of the world."

"Oh, yeah?" Lannon questioned. "It just may be, pal. This time they'll prove you shouldn't have been flying. They'll—"

"And they'll be right," Hill broke in, turning to face his aide squarely.

"Whatta you mean, Ed?" Lannon snapped with obvious panic. He wasn't prepared for Hill's remark. He could *not* understand his abrupt change in attitude. "We got to fight this thing, Ed," he pleaded. "We must—"

"All right, all right, Joe," Hill held up a hand. "Let's not go over it now. Let's just get out of here alive. Okay?"

Lannon was still stunned. He stared at Hill. "Ed, you don't seem to understand," he said finally. "This time you've got a national hero on your hands. And he's going to make one hell of a witness. By the time he gets through with you, you'll be out of flying and politics and anything else in sight."

"And that'd be bad, huh, Joe." Hill smiled.

"Christ, yes, Ed." Lannon shook his head. He simply couldn't believe what he was hearing from Hill. "What's with you? We can't let that happen. *I* won't let that happen. Not now. Not—"

"Oh, all right, Joe." Hill interrupted again, taking his aide firmly by the shoulders. "Get hold of yourself. Let it go. What's the point of discussing it now?"

"Uh, none, no point, uh, not now, Ed," Lannon stuttered. "I just want to keep the record straight. That's all."

"Fine, Joe, I understand," Hill said. "I've understood you for some time," he added, stepping back onto the wing of the Navion. "But for now," he continued, "let's try and figure out our best course of action, Joe. Determine how we're going to stay alive. Okay?"

"Right, Ed, we'll discuss it later," Lannon agreed finally, turning from Hill.

He took a few steps from the plane, his eyes studying two figures in the shade of nearby rocks. Lannon watched as Greg stood over a sitting Steve Austin, doctoring the facial burns the former astronaut had suffered during the in-flight turbulence.

"That's about it, Colonel. I flushed them out the best I could," Greg said easily, pressing gently around Steve Austin's right eye with a wad of gauze. "The right eye's badly inflamed with hardly any pupil. The left eye—well, it's totally discolored," he added, puzzled. "Is it artificial?"

"Yes," Steve answered casually, not wanting to arouse the young man's curiosity any further.

Greg wrapped gauze around Steve's head, making sure it was tight enough to keep sunlight out of the damaged eye. "Is that better?" he asked.

"Much better," Steve smiled. "Thank you, Greg. You'll make somebody a great doctor."

"Well, not much in this kit to work with," the boy demurred. "Now if you'd had snakebite, well, I could've really shown you some moves."

"I'd bet," Steve laughed.

"If old Doc Hill can be of further service," Greg returned the laugh, "just let us know. We make house calls."

"I'll keep that in mind," Steve said, turning his face in the direction of Greg's voice.

The two of them remained quiet for a moment, enjoying the shade. Then, cautiously, Steve asked, "How 'bout it, old Doc Hill, you think it's just temporary?"

"Sure," Greg answered quickly. "I read once about this—" He broke into his own words. "Look, Colonel, how do I know?" he continued, soberly. "All I know for sure is that you need a real doctor. And you need him today."

Steve nodded, accepting Greg's diagnosis of his condition. He'd been in tight spots before, and experience had taught him now was the time to think positive.

"What about your father, Greg? Think he has any ideas on how to get me to that real doctor today?"

"Don't know, Colonel," Greg answered, shaking his head. "Why don't you ask him? Here he is now."

Steve turned to face the approaching movement he heard easily. Although he'd only been blind for an hour, he was beginning to understand how sightless people managed so well. No sooner than Hill had moved into the shade and hunkered down beside him than Steve was acutely aware of Hill's sweaty odor.

"Well, how you doing?" he heard Hill ask.

"I've been better, General," he replied. "Any sign of Air Rescue?"

"No." Hill shook his head. "At least, not yet."

"Our doctor here," Steve waved in the general direction of Greg, "says I need medical attention. Want to give me our situation, straight?"

"Okay, straight," Hill agreed, picking up a rock and fingering it gently. "We're about one hundred miles off course in the middle of nowhere without a transmitter or an ELT." He paused, tossing the rock across the desert. "I'm afraid we have to wait until they find us."

"What's an ELT, Dad?"

"An emergency location transmitter."

"What about walking out, General?" Steve asked.

105

"Can't make it, Colonel. Nearest town is at least twenty miles."

"No roads, no highways nearby?"

"None, Colonel," Hill said flatly. "We're in the middle of the Cabeza Prieta National Wildlife Refuge."

"But, Dad, what are we going to do?"

"Wait for Air Rescue, son."

"How long will that take?" Greg persisted.

"I don't know, son. That weather we just came through," he said quietly, gesturing toward the thunderstorms in the distance. "It may be tomorrow before they can even start a search."

"Dad!" Greg threw his father a hard look. "He needs a doctor *now*."

"I know, Greg." Hill stared at the boy. "But I don't know what else we can do."

"General, what about flying out?" Steve asked.

"*Flying* out? You mean in the Navion?"

Steve nodded.

"No way, Colonel."

"We lose too much oil? That it?"

"No, that's not it," Hill explained. "I learned a long time ago to keep a couple of extra cans of oil on board."

"What is it, then?"

"The prop! I didn't kill the engine soon enough on the way in," Hill said disgustedly. "A tip is bent."

"Okay," Steve said. "We've got a busted oil line and a bent prop. What else?"

"*What else?*" Hill shook his head. "What more do you need, Colonel? Hell, that plane's not gonna fly with a bent prop. It would tear the engine right out of its mounts."

"I'll take care of the prop," Steve said. "Can you fix the oil line?"

"Sure, that's no problem," Hill answered, puzzled. "But there's not a tool on board that plane capable of unbending that—"

"Never mind, General," Steve broke in, "what about a takeoff strip?"

"Well, we'd have to clear rocks and brush along the old river bed," Hill answered, still baffled. "But with eight or nine hundred feet cleared to the north," he continued, thoughtfully, "we'd have a slope into the valley that should help."

"Good."

"But, Colonel, there're some pretty big rocks out there, and we sure as hell won't last long in this heat without water, and—"

"And we won't last at all if we just sit down and quit, right, General?"

Hill dropped his head. "I suppose you're right," he agreed finally. "There's not much chance Air Rescue will find us. At least, not today."

"No chance at all," Steve said, rising to his feet. "Now, with a little eyesight help from you people, I'll take care of the prop and the biggest rocks."

Hill shot a confused glance at Lannon. "This I must see for myself," he said flatly.

"Lead me to the plane, Greg," Steve said, extending his hand.

Moments later, while the others looked on in disbelief, Steve Austin's bionics hand explored the curvature of the damaged tip of the Navion's propeller. His bionics fingers squeezed the metal with extraordinary strength and he shouted, "Switch off?"

"Uh, yes." Hill confirmed. "Switch is off."

Steve's bionic fingers gripped with vise-like power. Hill started to speak, but held his words. He and the others simply could not believe what they saw. Without any tool of any kind, Steve Austin's hand slowly but surely moved the steel in the prop's tip, bending it back to its original shape.

They stared at the newly straightened propeller blade, astonished as Steve Austin's incredible fingers smoothed the steel surface as if they were flattening a sheet of kitchen foil on a baking tray.

"How's that, Senator?" Steve asked. "Is she straight?"

Hill stepped forward, quickly glancing at the others. They were all dumbfounded. He managed to speak. "Yes, uh, Colonel, it's straight."

"Be sure. Check it carefully," Steve told him. "We can't afford to have an unbalanced prop."

"As they say, Colonel, it's close enough for government work." He shook his head in amazement. "Just how in God's name did you do that?"

Steve took a step backward and stared in the direction of Hill's voice. "Senator," he began, choosing not to address the other man at this point by his military rank. "Two years ago you got Oscar Goldman six million dollars for a secret project. I was the project. They gave me some expensive new parts."

"But, the strength . . . your strength, Colonel," Hill said, finding it difficult to believe. "No man is that strong."

"It's the new parts," Steve answered. "They come in handy at times. Like paying Oscar's old debts."

"Uh-huh." Hill nodded. "I assume that . . . ah . . . whatever it was they did to you is still classified?"

"Top secret," Steve said firmly.

"We understand, Colonel. We can and *will* keep your secret," he said, turning to face Joe Lannon and Greg to be sure his promise was understood.

"Good." Steve smiled. "Now let's get on with it. How much runway did you say you needed for a take-off?"

"Well," Hill brought a hand to his chin, "to be safe, we'd better clear nine hundred feet."

"Nine hundred feet it is," Steve nodded. "Which way is the wind?"

"What there is of it, it's out of the north," Hill answered. "In our favor, toward the slope."

"Well, be thankful for small favors," Steve said, turning in the general direction of the others.

"Greg," he ordered, "pace off nine hundred feet to the north. Put some sort of marker there."

"Right, Colonel Austin," Greg answered, hurrying off.

"Senator, can you get started on that oil line?"

"Sure, Colonel, right away."

"Where's Joe?"

"Uh, here, Colonel," Lannon answered numbly.

"Come on, guide me out," Steve smiled. "We've got some rocks to move."

CHAPTER TWELVE

Four hours passed, and the strip of desert was nearly cleared of rocks and brush from the Navion to where Greg had paced off nine hundred feet. There he'd tied his T-shirt to one of his father's fishing poles and planted it at the crest of the slope. All appeared nearly ready as the four men labored, sweating, trying to ignore their thirst.

Senator Ed Hill had repaired the oil line in quick order, and, after adding two reserve cans of oil to the engine, he'd joined the others in moving rocks and brush.

They worked feverishly while never losing their amazement at the rapid pace set by a blinded Steve Austin. The six-million-dollar man moved through the makeshift airstrip like a machine, uprooting small bushes, flipping the largest of the rocks with deceptive ease.

But Steve Austin was not aware of their amazement. He was deep in thought of the last time he'd moved about a dusty landscape in search of rocks. His trek across the lunar surface had been far more comfortable than the chore he was about this day. On the moon he'd been cool inside his bulky space suit, sipping water when he desired it from the built-in supply, and, with only one-sixth of earth's gravity slowing his efforts,

110

moving about the lunar landscape with the speed and agility of a lightweight kangaroo.

Of course, he smiled to himself, there was something to be said for the ability of his bionics legs. They gave him great speed and strength in spite of earth's gravity. Far more than he'd had with his former legs in the lesser gravity of the moon. But that was another time, most certainly another place, and now his task was to hurl the rocks clear of the only ship that could take them back to civilization.

He moved about the desert beneath the broiling sun with the others guiding him to and from each object to be cleared. Several times he'd heard the distant sound of jets and had stopped to listen. Nothing in the air came close to them. Their only hope was to fly the Navion out, through the weather front to Luke.

Blinded, he moved carefully, cautiously, the desert floor he trod a mixture of clumps of sand, hard rock, brush, and God knew what else. Sometimes his foot would stab into an obstacle and he'd stumble forward, reeling as he fought for his balance.

He'd long since felt the heat baking him, slowly roasting his exposed skin to a deep red hue. He'd tied his handkerchief around his neck and he was thankful for the gauze Greg had tied in a band around his head. It not only kept sunlight out of his injured eye, but sweat and grime as well.

Suddenly he was aware of his own fatigue and realized how tired the others must be. They didn't have the benefit of his bionics legs to move them about their work. Their lungs and limbs couldn't withstand the same torture.

Steve halted his movement and held up his hands. "All right," he shouted. "Five-minute break!"

He heard no complaints from the others and, without their help, he managed to find shade. He sucked air deeply into his lungs as he sat down beside a row of tall rocks. Near him he heard the others collapse in exhaustion, gasping for air.

111

They were all now content simply to rest, to give their tortured lungs the chance to breathe without dragging dust and sand through their throats.

Steve sat quietly, imagining what it must look like around them. He recalled how Greg had described their location to him, and he pictured the river that had once flowed through this wasteland, that had sliced a deep furrow in the ground to create the sheer earthen canyon wall. Suddenly he felt a breeze, the first wind, it seemed, since they'd begun clearing the strip. He could *hear* sand lifted into the air by the breeze as something new, making a sound surprisingly like dry, powdered snow racing over the frozen surface of the Arctic.

He thought about things crisp and cool and imagined what it would be like if they had winds on the moon. That fine powdery surface, whipped up and cast over the cindery, dusty surface. Much like this sun-baked hell, he mused.

Well, you can only go to the moon once, Austin, he reminded himself, thankful to have been one of only twelve men to walk on that faraway surface.

He turned, aware of movement. "Colonel Austin, uh," he heard Greg stutter as the lad approached. "I've been wanting to ask you something."

He sat up, facing the direction of the voice. "Sure, buddy, what is it?"

"Well, I'm certain you've been asked this many times before," Greg said quietly. "I was just wondering if you'd mind me asking it again?"

Steve smiled. "Not at all, Greg. Shoot."

"What I'd like to know, Colonel, is . . . uh . . . I mean . . . uh . . ." he stuttered even more, finding the words difficult. "What I'm trying to ask is, what's it like seeing the earth, our world, from way out there, from the moon?"

Steve relaxed and leaned back against the rock. "Of course, the very first time is the greatest, Greg," he answered, beginning the story as he had so many times before. "And every time we had a chance to

112

look at the earth after that, we did. And when we took the time to *really* look, to try to understand what we were seeing, well, it was just damned overwhelming."

Steve lifted his arms with his right hand gesturing in a curving motion. "When you come around the moon, this dead, cratered world," he continued, "and suddenly over the horizon, a quarter of a million miles away, it's there."

"Home!"

"Right," Steve smiled. "That's how you think of it, Greg. Like the word never had meaning before. It rolls through space, this beautiful blue world floating against the blackest black there ever was, and you feel you could look around the other side of the earth. The pictures, the films you've seen, they don't mean anything because they're flat. But you see it as a round ball, and you hold up both hands by the window of the spacecraft, and you can cup the world in your hands and . . . and well, all of a sudden you feel how fragile it is . . . You finally realize it's all there is, all we have. As you said, Greg, it's *home*. Understand?"

"I understand, Colonel," Greg said quietly. "Thank you," he added, standing up, looking about him, surveying the work yet to be done. "If I'm going to have any part in preserving the . . . uh . . . no, our home," he smiled, "we'd better get on with building ourselves a runway."

"Right," Steve agreed, moving to his feet. "Let's get cracking," he called in the direction of Hill and Lannon.

Senator Ed Hill lay flat on his back in the desert dust. With the call from Steve Austin he rolled to an elbow, halting long enough to suck another deep breath of cool air into his lungs before sitting up. At age fifty-four, and twenty pounds overweight, his physical endurance was nearly spent. But he realized the necessity for their physical torture, and he started

113

to his feet only to feel Joe Lannon's hand restrain him.

He turned to his aide and studied the desperate look on Lannon's face.

"I can't believe this," Lannon said disgustedly, nodding toward Steve Austin. "We're knocking ourselves out to take him back. So he can blow us both apart."

Hill jerked his arm free from Lannon's hand and rose to his feet.

"I mean it's all backwards, isn't it?" his aide asked as he stood up. "What we should be doing is figuring a way to *leave* him here."

"Joe!" Hill shouted. "Knock it off!"

"Well, that would be a solution, wouldn't it? And easily explained. We could say he died in the crash."

Hill spun about and grabbed his aide by the shoulders. "Are you out of your mind, Joe?"

Lannon twisted free of Hill's grip. "Look, Ed," he spat. "I'll find a way, you don't have to be involved—"

"Dammit, Joe!" Hill shook his head. "I can't believe this! You're really serious!"

"Damn right I'm serious," Lannon snapped with heated anger. "I've got a lifetime invested in you, Ed, and—"

The sharp movement of Hill's hand startled Joe Lannon and halted his words as he stared at the raised fist, at the arm poised to unleash the blow. But the fist never moved, never struck out toward his face. Instead, it dropped lifelessly back to the Senator's side.

Ed Hill sighed disgustedly, gripping Lannon by the shoulders once again. "Joe, pull yourself together," he said firmly. "Don't ever suggest anything like this to me again. Understand?"

He didn't wait for an answer. He walked away from his aide to help his son and Steve Austin clear the takeoff strip.

Joe Lannon stood watching the others at work. Greg and Senator Hill lifted and stumbled with tortured

114

movements. Steve Austin assaulted the rocks and brush like the machine he was. Lannon spat from a dry mouth into the desert dust and wiped the back of his hand across his parched lips. We'll get out of here, all right, he thought angrily. And for what? To face a Board of Inquiry just so Colonel Steve Austin, former astronaut and national hero, can be our chief accuser? Yeah, that's for what; he shook his head disgustedly.

His heart wasn't in it, but he moved toward the work area. His steps were slow and meaningless. He'd never seen Ed Hill like this before. He simply could not understand the Senator's reaction to their predicament. What must be done was very clear to him. They were about to be exiled from politics for life, a problem that could be remedied wtih only one solution. Why in God's name couldn't Ed see that?

He slapped at a tumbleweed and gave it a kick, booting it clear of the takeoff strip. He began his work well ahead of the others, gladly keeping his distance. Could it be, he frowned, that Ed simply didn't give a damn? This is the end of it all and he just doesn't care? Well, he'd damn well better! He'll be lucky to finish his present term in office, he thought. There sure as hell won't be any delegates knocking his door down to haul him off to the convention floor for the second spot on the ticket. That's for damn sure.

He started to reach for a rock, to pick it up. The way Ed's been acting—

BRRRRRRRRRRRRRRT!

Joe Lannon froze, startled by a sound he'd heard only once before in his life. An unmistakable sound. The machine-gun screech of the reptile world.

In spite of the heat, chills moved in waves up his back and sprouted with dampness on his face. He moved cautiously backward, ever so slowly, and—

BRRRRRRRRRRRRRRT!

There it was again! The sound of warning and fury coiled at the end of a giant mainspring about to explode free.

115

But he too was free. There was distance between him and the rattler coiled in the shade of the rock, and he waited for his nerves to settle, for the chills to subside. Then it was obvious. His chance. Their chance to rid themselves of the one man who could and would destroy everything they'd worked for.

Lannon turned slowly, staring at the rapid movements of the man-machine. "Colonel Austin," he called, "I need your help on this one!"

Steve stopped, turning in the direction of Lannon's voice. "What's your problem, Joe?"

"This rock, Colonel, it's too big for me to handle."

"Right," Steve acknowledged. "Which way?"

"Over here," Lannon said easily. "Keep coming."

"Anything in my way?"

"Nothing, just follow my voice," Lannon told him, guiding the unsuspecting cyborg toward the rock where the rattler waited, coiled. "That's it, Colonel, just a few more steps."

There was no lack of confidence in Steve's strides as he walked briskly toward the sound of Lannon's voice. He reached the area without the slightest warning of the rock and the death coiled beneath it. His right foot jammed itself beneath the boulder's sharp edge and as he tumbled wildly forward, Steve heard the sound, that voice alien to everything else in the animal kingdom.

BRRRRRRRRRRRRRT! The snake sent its warning as Austin knew the ground was coming up to meet his helpless fall. His bionics arm shot through air, cutting like lightning in the direction of the rattler, his sensors telling him instantly he'd found the coiling target.

The rattler struck once and Steve knew the snake had missed. In a flash the squirming reptile was hurled upward, away from that part of his body that was human flesh.

Joe Lannon's eyes were wide with disbelief at the scene before him. He had only a split second to see the outstretched rattler hurtling toward him. No time

116

to react. No time to panic. Only an instant to see the white underside of the snake, to see fangs protruding from a gaping mouth before the rattler landed with a smacking force across his neck.

Wildly he brushed the cold reptile away, and for the briefest of moments he was safe.

But he wasn't!

At his feet he saw the rattler coil, saw the swift strike of the head, felt the snake's sharp fangs puncture his leg below the knee. There was little left for him to do but scream as he stumbled backward and sank to his knees.

"Greg?" he heard Steve Austin call. "Something's happened to Joe!"

"I'm coming, Colonel Austin," he heard the boy answer as he felt the venom flaming through his system.

"The rattler . . ." Lannon's voice was a terrified gurgle.

"Rattlesnake, Greg," Steve yelled, "bring your first aid kit."

"Right, Colonel!"

Lannon lay quietly, watching the rattlesnake slide off into the desert. Finally he looked up at Steve Austin. "I'm sorry, Colonel," he said weakly.

"Sorry? About what?"

"The snake!"

Steve stared in his blindness, puzzled. He dismissed it from his mind as he heard Greg arrive.

"Where'd he get you, Mr. Lannon?"

"Below the knee, Greg," he said, pointing to his right leg.

Greg turned to his father, who had followed him. "Dad, help me get him in a sitting position," he said. "We want to keep his heart above the wound."

"Right, son," Hill said, lifting Lannon. "You're going to be all right, Joe," he added quickly. "Greg knows what he's doing. He's okay when it comes to things like this," he assured his aide.

Lannon nodded and watched as Greg moved without hesitation.

117

First the lad split the leg of his trousers above the knee, exposing the twin punctures in the skin where the rattler had sunk its fangs. He applied a constricting band four inches above the bite and took the blade from the snakebite kit. Carefully he made two shallow incisions, running from each fang puncture to the venom deposit below the wound. Quickly he applied the suction cup to the area and began withdrawing venom.

Senator Hill watched while Steve Austin listened. Neither man said a word until several minutes had passed. It seemed Greg would never stop.

"How about it, Greg?" Hill asked finally. "How much longer?"

Without stopping the suction action, Greg looked up. "To be sure, this procedure takes at least thirty minutes, Dad," he explained. "And out here we'd better be sure."

"What can we do, Greg?" Steve spoke up.

"Well, Colonel, I should be able to get a lot of the venom out," he said, "but Mr. Lannon, just like you, needs a hospital."

"You'll be at that for thirty minutes?"

"Just about," Greg nodded.

"That should give us time to get the Navion ready," he said, turning in the direction of Hill. "How about it, Senator? Think we've cleared enough runway to get out of here?"

Hill studied the takeoff strip. They were a good hundred feet short. He'd have to move the marker to where the strip had been finished. But with a little luck the Navion could make it.

"I'm with you, Colonel," he said, taking Steve by the arm. He couldn't resist a momentary pause for another proud look at his son.

CHAPTER THIRTEEN

Senator Ed Hill looked about the cabin. In the rear Greg had the unconscious Joe Lannon strapped securely in his seat. Up front, to his right, a blinded Steve Austin sat waiting, his seat belt pulled tightly across his lap. All seemed to be ready. All but him.

He had learned many things this day, two of which he could not ignore. First, General Edwin J. Hill should *not* fly. Second, he *must*. He was still the only game in town.

He shifted in his seat and checked his own belt. *You can't make any mistakes. None. Not even a small one. There's no room for mistakes. There's hardly any room for the airplane* . . .

Hill laughed at himself for that last thought. Well, thank God he still had some sense of humor left in him. That could also be spelled out as perspective. A man had to meet reality head on, but he could also be so grim he'd get tunnel vision. Amazing how a few fleeting thoughts could clear his head. It was like a fresh breeze through his mind. Just that one touch of being able to regard himself with wry humor. It helped. But what he'd thought was also terribly true. There wasn't *any* room for—how did they always spell that out?

No margin for error. They—whoever *they* were—

couldn't have nailed it down more neatly. No margin for error.

Hill took a deep breath and forced himself to think logically. Think of *everything*. Go through every step in his mind. Leave nothing out.

The Navion, now. They'd lined up at the very end of the impromptu airstrip they'd cleared out of the desert floor. The tail of the airplane was backed up over rough and rocky ground. They'd pushed it back to that point. The main gear stood on the very lip of usable runway. Hill made a sour face. Calling this goat path they'd cleared of rocks and shrubs a "runway" was the height of optimism.

Good; he needed to remind himself about that. With a man in the back seat being torn apart through his system from snake venom, with another man to his right so blinded he couldn't see a damned thing, and with himself suffering—no matter how well he kept that secret from the others, he couldn't keep it from himself—the torment of the damned in his own head, he might as well be optimistic.

They trembled on the brink of total disaster. All four of them. And—*dammit, Hill,* he reprimanded himself, *get with it and stay with what you're doing.* Yeah; that was what it was all about. Concentrate; that was the trick. Concentrate on every last detail.

He reviewed their position in his mind. Every last inch of runway was being used. Okay; dismiss that. No improvement there. He didn't like the wind that much. What there was of it had changed slightly. It was quartering from one side. Oh, they still had an into-the-wind factor that would help to reduce the takeoff run, but it would sure help if it had stayed right down their nose. Well, it hadn't, he snapped at himself. Okay, he judged it as best he could from blowing dust and from the fluttering T-shirt Greg had tied onto the fishing pole that marked the end of the runway. He thought about it for a moment. He'd keep slight back pressure on the yoke, keep the nosewheel from plowing into the dirt, keep the angle of

120

attack of the wings to the absolute minimum to reduce drag. More than anything else he needed lift from those wings, and the only way to get that lift was speed. None of this smooth takeoff nonsense.

Okay, this was it. "Everybody ready?" he asked as if they had a choice.

"All set back here, Dad."

"Same here," Steve Austin said. "Fire her up."

The propeller turned a couple of times and the engine coughed, then caught, whining with its steady rising pitch. Hill watched the fuel pressure and flow and temperatures. The Navion was alive.

"How's the oil pressure?" Steve asked.

"Holding. It looks good," Hill told him. "I'll make a quick run through the checklist."

"Right," Steve said. "Let me know if I can help. Even a blind copilot is better than no copilot at all."

"No argument," Hill answered as he began going over the gauges carefully.

Oil pressure in the green. Oil temperature in the green. No sweat. The two reserve cans of oil were sufficient. Suction pump okay. The amount of fuel they had in the tanks didn't mean a damn at this moment, but fuel pressure most certainly did. It was right where it belonged. He reached over suddenly and turned off the radios. It was more psychology than anything else, but he didn't want to drain any energy from this machine that wasn't needed for the takeoff. Of a sudden he stared at the panel, then moved his eyes to the fuel controls. My God; it would have been hell if he'd tried the takeoff on the wrong tank! But everything was where it belonged with the tank selector.

He went through the checklist in his mind and then followed the basic procedures. Controls. He moved the yoke full forward and back, rotated it full left and full right. There was always that remote chance that something might have snagged. The yoke moved smoothly through the control test. Again he went through the instruments, scanning the panel. It was all

121

in the green. He pushed forward on the mixture control to be absolutely certain it was all the way in. The same for carburetor heat. Even a smidgin of carb heat on takeoff could rob them of power. He rechecked the fuel selector, glanced at the tank gauges, again checked pressure feed. Flaps. He set them only for lift. No drag, no drag, he kept repeating to himself. Trim. He thought about that for a moment, then rolled in a bit of extra nose-up trim. Better to fight the controls a bit once they broke ground, because when he came back on the yoke he wanted nothing left to chance.

He checked the canopy lock. He could have used the air rushing past the open canopy to cool them off, but that meant drag. He triple-checked it to be sure it was locked. His seat. Hell, seats had come loose before under takeoff acceleration and bouncing over rough ground. He moved his weight back and forth. Locked; no problems there.

Sweat poured down his forehead, stinging his eyes. He wiped his mouth with the back of his hand. *Get with it, Hill*, an inner voice growled at him.

There's nothing left to do but fly!

Or . . . *try* to fly.

He forced that nonsense from his mind. He was *going* to fly and that was all there was to it, and one never knew—positive thinking might just help them get off the ground before they ran out of runway and went crunching into the boonies beyond.

He brought the throttle forward steadily. There was a moment when his attention wandered from the airplane to the dying man in the back seat and the blinded man to his right, and, again angrily, he forced all that crap from his mind. Because it *was* crap. Sentimentality about anything else save the airplane is not only stupid when you should be concentrating—it can be lethal.

And with that final thought he blotted out everything else but what he was doing and what he yet had to do. His feet went down on the top half of the rudder pedals to lock the brakes solidly. His left hand gripped the yoke firmly, and the throttle kept moving under his right hand until it was all the way against the stop. A fast look to check manifold pressure and RPM, and everything was wound around to the right as far as it would go. He pushed forward on the yoke, holding the nose wheel hard against the ground, and when he knew there was nothing left but that screaming engine waiting to grab air with the prop, he snapped pressure away from the brakes, eased off on the yoke, got both heels on the floorboards and let her go.

The Navion had been trembling wildly from remaining in one place while the prop blasted air over the wings and fuselage and tail. Now the trembling was replaced with shaking, but it was the rumble and sway of movement, and Hill felt the shocks of the nose wheel slamming up and down in its oleo strut to the full play, transmitting the blows through the fuselage. To hell with that; to hell with everything except what was happening in front of him.

The Navion rushed away from its starting position, fighting for speed along the makeshift runway which stretched across the rough, dry river bed, reached to the marker where the earth suddenly dropped into a steep slope and fell toward a wide valley bordered by a mountain ridge.

The airplane rocked wildly from the uneven ground, but that didn't matter a damn. He was in a strange world of thundering, rushing movement, and his mind was working faster than the Navion, getting ahead of things that were happening, trying to anticipate, to be ready before anything went wrong. He applied right rudder to compensate for the engine torque of takeoff. Damn that wind . . . it was from their left, and he had to keep an absolutely straight line. They didn't have any room to spare on either side of that wide gear. If he drifted from the narrow runway he'd tear off a wheel or crumple a gear, and he brought in left aileron with the yoke. The yoke rotating to the left would help

123

overcome the wind force from that side and keep him rolling true.

And then he seemed to be in a world of soft, mushy cloud, as time dragged its heels on him. He knew they were picking up speed swiftly, they were accelerating, his hand had the throttle hard against the stop, but everything seemed to be happening with impossible, maddening slowness.

It was a race. A race to get airspeed—enough speed to get lift from the wings before they ran out of the last foot of usable ground. If they didn't make it, that was the name of the game. But dammit, they'd make it, he swore to himself.

Brush and sand and rocks hurtled by, the Navion rocking wildly now. He had enough speed so that the ground effect of the wings tried to ease them into the air. The danger was that a bump could ease them into the air, but that was a killer, because they'd only settle back to the ground once more and they didn't have enough room for that kind of game. He needed all his speed in one great, swift gulp of hurtling over the ground, because when he committed it would be total.

The fluttering T-shirt rushed at him from one side of his vision. Concentrate on that marker . . . concentrate. Judge by the cloth. Aim just to the side of it, down the rough strip, getting all the speed there was. Squeeze it out of the damned plane, out of the prop. Speed, precious speed for precious lift from those wings.

His every instinct screamed for him to come back on the yoke, to haul the Navion into the air. He could almost feel the runway left hurtling from his grasp, feel the rough ground and rocks and brush beyond the fluttering T-shirt waiting to tear up the gear and—

He timed it perfectly. At the last instant, with nothing in the world directly before them save disaster, he jerked back on the yoke. With the speed he had now the Navion didn't take off.

It lunged into the air like a thing berserk.

But Hill knew this was an invitation to a crash, because when he came back on the yoke, snatching the airplane into the air, he had barely enough speed to struggle above the ground. What happened now was absolutely critical, and in swift motion he went forward on the yoke to lower the nose, to kill drag and to help build up speed. At the same instant his right hand banged against the gear lever and he pawed it into the UP position.

Several things were happening at the same long, intolerable instant. They were in the air—barely. Speed was starting to slip away. He cleaned up the Navion by tucking up the gear, and when every instinct yelled for altitude he went forward on the yoke and dropped back toward the ground.

If he could just get some help from ground effect . . .

The Navion wobbled drunkenly, *but the speed was holding.* Holding them clear of the sickening view only a few feet beneath them—cactus, rocks, and brush startlingly close as the small plane reached the valley and plunged toward the mountain ridge. Still, he needed more airspeed. But he was left without a choice. The jagged hills rushed toward them and he rolled the yoke to the right, kicked in right rudder, and the Navion's wing tip kissed a Joshua tree. It was the only way to move and Hill took it, wrestling the controls to roll out of the shallow turn and keep the wings level until the airspeed indicator began to crawl around its dial.

He followed the dry river bed that snaked its way through the valley, and the airspeed needle began to slide more to the right, the controls were becoming stronger, the Navion was responding as they plunged forward, the big propeller only feet away from striking the rock-strewn ground, and there was enough speed—a shade above barely, *but enough*—to come back gently, very gently, on the yoke, and to ease into a shallow climb.

His breath exploded from him.

God, every moment beyond that sort of thing . . . you *knew* what it was to be alive.

His thoughts sobered. They had made it—but the

storm waited for them. Directly ahead. All around them.

He concentrated on the moment. The Growler Mountains ahead. He knew he should be coming back on the RPM. The prop was fairly screaming out there, but he waited. Let it run hot for a little while. He didn't care if the damned thing never worked again, *after* this flight.

But he found he didn't have to beat it to death. They were flying solidly now, and the ground below kept falling away. He eased off on RPM and power, but kept the Navion in a high-performance climb, and the foothills of the Growlers rushing toward them kept falling below their altitude, and then they were clear, the Navion rocking in turbulence from the storm waiting for them.

Hill looked at the dark, ominous clouds. *All right, you bastards*, he said to himself, *you're next.*

CHAPTER FOURTEEN

Sergeant Jill Denby rubbed her shoulder muscles. Her neck hurt, and she'd had a nagging ache in her lower back for hours. To say nothing of the sandpaper roughness of her eyes. Staring at a radarscope isn't the best treatment for your vision, and the young WAF had been at it on a steady basis ever since the civilian aircraft disappeared into serious weather beyond the Growler Mountains.

The radar crews and air traffic controllers who manned the Ground Control Approach Radar Facility at Luke Air Force Base were getting accustomed to Jill Denby's sense of duty. Since she had alerted Major Phillips, the operations officer, to a potential disaster situation, several things had happened. Operations had queried the FAA about any missing aircraft. A broad-canvas check was about all they could do. And then the pieces began to fit, and when they did, a chill swept through the staff on duty.

A civilian aircraft, Navion 4372K, had departed San Diego for Luke AFB. Aboard the machine were four people. Colonel Steve Austin, Senator—and also Brigadier General—Edwin J. Hill, and two civilians.

Jill Denby and the others working with her could come to only one conclusion. No other aircraft were missing—or, at least, reported missing. Until they learned otherwise, they must assume the only aircraft missing was Navion 4372K.

Major Phillips immediately flashed the word to San Diego, where Steve Austin had last met with Oscar Goldman from OSO. It didn't take long to start official dust blowing from *that* direction. Goldman obviously carried a lot of weight, for the radar room received word that the OSO man was already on his way by private jet to Luke AFB.

Sergeant Jill Denby was at her radar console when Major Phillips came into the control room with Goldman in tow. They went directly to her scope position.

"Anything new, Sergeant?" asked the major.

She turned with a blank expression and shook her head slowly. "No, sir," she said. "I wish . . . No, sir. Nothing at all."

"This is Mr. Goldman," Phillips told her. "From OSO."

She turned to Goldman. "Yes, sir." She didn't know what else to say. Goldman nodded his greeting.

"Sergeant Denby is the controller I spoke about to you before, Mr. Goldman," Phillips went on smoothly. "She's the one who's been putting together all the pieces since that first radar contact."

Goldman showed sudden interest. His eyes went over and through her. "How long has it been, Sergeant?" His voice was gravelly, almost strained.

"Just over six hours, sir."

"Did the blip go off scope?"

"No, sir, it—"

"I meant to ask if you lost contact while it was still in range."

"Oh. No, sir. I was able to follow to full range."

"You mean the aircraft was still moving, still flying? When you lost track?"

"Yes, sir. It was moving southeast. No question about it being in the air, Mr. Goldman," she assured him. "But we haven't had any additional contact since that time."

Goldman looked at Phillips. "We've got to assume

they went down." He gestured at the scope. "At least we know in what direction they were flying and the most likely area to search. How soon can you get started on that, Major?"

Phillips shook his head. "I'd like to start right now, sir," he told Goldman. "But in this weather? Not a chance. From what we can see, the stuff is close to the ground. We wouldn't dare send our people into those mountains, and—"

"How soon?" Goldman snapped.

"The moment the weather clears, sir. *The* moment."

"I understand. Of course." Goldman rubbed his neck. "Sorry, major. I didn't mean to—"

"No sweat, sir."

"We'll just have to wait, won't we," Goldman said. It was a statement and not a question.

"Yes, sir. But the crews will be standing by and ready to roll as soon as weather permits." The major turned to Jill Denby. "Sergeant, thanks for everything you've done here. You nailed this one neatly. You can break as soon as I get relief in here to replace you."

The girl seemed startled by his words. "Major? Please, I'd like to stay on. It feels like . . . I mean, you understand, sir? It feels like my airplane . . . uh . . . my people out there."

Goldman showed sudden new interest in her. "Sergeant, I appreciate that." A smile showed briefly on his face. "I like your style, Jill." He turned to the officer. "Major, I'd like to wait here with her, if I may."

"Of course. Some coffee help?"

"That it would. For the both of us," he said with a glance at Jill Denby. He moved a chair beside her, and they both turned to the radar scope.

It stared blankly back at them.

On the Navion everything was going to hell fast. The plane punched through growing turbulence over the Growler Mountains. Nothing the airplane or the pilot couldn't handle—not at that moment, anyway—but ahead of them lay the line of towering thunderstorms,

129

the massive wall of cloud mountains with all its sight-robbing mists, with rain and turbulence and lightning, and God knew what else. Any other time Ed would have turned back from that threatening mass. But not now. Not with two men critically hurt. Simple, really.

Don't fly—and one man will certainly be dead soon. The other may never again see.

Fly—and risk killing them all. But far better, judged Hill, to take a chance than to do nothing.

He flexed his arms and legs, and his left hand took a firmer grip on the yoke, with his right hand ready at any moment to chop or add power if necessary. Hill grunted to himself. What the hell, he'd done this plenty of times before in his long and eventful flying career. Just a plunge through line center and—

His thoughts of the past vanished as grayness enveloped them. Hill concentrated on the panel. Airspeed, rate of climb or descent, needle and ball, above all the gyro horizon. Heading, and—

Gray light flashed about them. They'd punched through the first heavy cloud. It hadn't been bad at all. Nothing more than a few light jabs from the storm gods all about them. But the gods could be nasty . . .

A massive wall towered above them. Plenty of room around this one. Hill rolled the Navion to the left, sliding the machine through clear airspace that let them get around that particular cumulus buildup. It could be a bitch inside one of those things. He had no way of judging turbulence or hail or freezing rain. He knew the thing was a powerhouse of crackling energy, because he could *see* the lightning bolts flashing through the mists. Besides, there was only one way to judge a thunderstorm, and no matter how you spelled it, it always came out *bad*.

He was able to continue their flight this way for a while—picking and threading a needle among the huge cloud mountains, managing to stay out of the really rough stuff. At least for now. And the approach control signal from Luke was coming in loud and clear, increasing in signal strength the closer they flew toward their objective.

That was the end of the good news. The weather was getting worse and the openings between storm clouds were getting pretty damned scarce, and then there was no way to go around anything. Now they were forced to fly through, and they raced from gray skies to darkness as the Navion plunged into heavy rain. The noise within the small plane had become a roaring hammer of sound. The thunder of the engine and the howl of wind seemed to gain in intensity as rain smashed at the windshield, drummed in sheets against the canopy, and beat a blasting tattoo against the wings and fuselage. The airplane groaned and creaked as turbulence sent it wallowing and skidding through the air, twisting metal and straining the ship.

Hill strained to see the instruments. Finally he remembered the panel lights, but in the wild blows of turbulent air, demanding his steady attention to the controls, he pawed and fumbled until he found the proper switch and spun it to the right for full intensity. It didn't help much, and the combination of poor light from outside and dim panel lights, as well as the sweat blinding him, made it pretty much of a mess.

God, what a way to go . . . a dying man in the back and a blinded one in the front seat with him, and his own kid gambling his life on a father who was near to some sort of panic, barely able to see, worrying every moment of the time if he'd be struck with this malady —of which the others knew nothing! Well, at least Greg was doing some good in the back seat, where he held the unconscious form of Joe Lannon, wiping the perspiration from his face, trying to do *anything* to help.

He *had* to hang on. They were getting closer every minute. Hill studied the panel, unaware he was talking aloud, vocalizing his thoughts. "On course," he murmured. "Heading . . . um . . . just a shade east of north . . . five degrees." He looked at the airspeed indicator. "Holding one eighty. We're getting there. Eighty miles to go and—"

131

To his right, Steve Austin was reacting, not to his voice, but to the weariness in his tone. A sound that brought the blinded man fully alert. "Senator? You all right?"

Steve had been holding his emotions in check. A man who's done his own flying all his life, from a local grass field to the moon, can hardly sit in a jolting, rocking plane—even if he's blind—without something tearing at his insides. And now to hear that voice, coming apart at the seams—

"I'm doing fine, just fine," Hill reassured him hastily. "It's hot in here, that's all. One day we'll get some decent vents in this damned machine."

Steve Austin didn't answer. It didn't matter if he believed what Hill had told him. What could he, Austin, do about anything?

At his side, Ed Hill felt the perspiration soaking his body. Sweat pooled in the hollow of his neck, collected under his armpits and ran down his sides. Because now there was no getting away from the storm gods. They were everywhere, sending fists of sudden violence against the Navion. Updrafts hurled them wildly higher, and, just as quickly as Hill fought to regain control of an airplane standing on its wing and shooting skywards, a howling river of air slammed them back toward the ground far below. They weren't flying any more so much as they struggled through unceasing violence. Again and again Hill blinked in pain as lightning speared the sky before them, jabbing savage light into his eyes. For long and terrible moments afterward, light-blinded, he saw the panel through misty and troubled vision.

A hammer blow of turbulence sent them tumbling off to his left. Panic stabbed through Hill as his eyes blurred. This had been his greatest fear, and like some invisible wraith taking shape within his body, he felt the steady onslaught of the enveloping darkness that had been such a terror in the past. He rubbed his eyes frantically and squinted at the instrument panel. Oh, God, it was happening, and he couldn't stop it. There

132

wasn't any panel before him. Only a streaming blur, a mishmash of light and shadow. Another attack . . .

The same as it had been before the crash . . . The same as it had been only hours before . . . It was happening again, only now they were trapped, prisoners in a storm with turbulence and rain and lightning and blindness for bars and he was the only pilot on board who could see and—

He fought desperately to hold it off. He shook his head wildly from side to side and pawed at his eyes. He—he couldn't think. But he had to—what? He tried to remember. Abruptly his hand shot forward, groping for the mike. His fumbling pushed it from its latch and knocked it to the floor.

"Austin! Colonel Austin . . . Steve . . . help . . . help me—"

Steve Austin was rigid in his seat, trying to understand what was happening. There was no mistaking the blind panic now in Hill's voice. Instinctively Steve's hands groped before him. "What's wrong, General?" No answer. Steve's voice was louder, demanding. "Dammit, speak to me, General!"

Hill had become totally disoriented. "The mike . . . I need to . . . where's the goddamned mike!"

Steve's left hand brushed along the panel and found the latch. "It couldn't have gone far, Ed," he said, more calmly now. "Probably dropped by your feet." His hand reached out and grasped Hill's right arm. "Why do you want the mike? We don't have a transmitter, remember?"

No answer came. What Steve Austin couldn't see was a rigid, frozen General Edwin J. Hill. The man was sitting well back in his seat, his eyes unblinking. Absolutely still.

Paralyzed by his attack.

Sergeant Jill Denby, Oscar Goldman by her side, studied the radar scope. The minutes were dragging, and—"Oh, Lord," she said suddenly, her voice a hoarse whisper. "We've got a target! See? There? I

133

have contact, Mr. Goldman! Right there! Fifty miles and . . . and . . . closing!"

"Good girl," Goldman said. "Stay with it. I'll get the major."

"Damn you . . . answer me!" Nothing. Steve's hands groped along the man to his side, feeling. What the hell was wrong with Hill? He wouldn't speak and—

Steve's fingers touched Hill's open eyes. In that instant Steve realized that something, somehow, had either killed or frozen Hill. *There was no reflex to Steve's fingers touching the eyeballs of the other man.* But he didn't have much time to think about it. The touch of Steve's hands and the continuing turbulence was enough to send Hill slumping over the control yoke before his body. The Navion jerked as if stung by the sudden forward movement of the yoke. By the sudden change of pressure on his own body, the feel of the yoke being too far forward, even to his blinded touch, the sudden growing scream of the wind past the airplane, he knew they were in a dive.

And he knew that, blinded or not, he had to bring the Navion out of its plunge or—

Steve's left hand found the throttle in the center of the console. He had to kill power, slow them down. He yanked back on the throttle, felt the engine roar drop. He grabbed for the yoke to haul it back. With his left hand, awkwardly, he pulled the slumping form away from the yoke.

"Greg!" Steve shouted. "Your father! Get him straight in his seat! Keep him off the controls! Quick!"

He heard the youngster gasping for breath. But the pressure was off the yoke. Steve brought in power, slowly, steadily.

"Greg, can you see the panel?"

"Uh, yes, sir."

"*Read the gauges, Greg.* You know the gyro horizon?"

"Uh, yes, I—"

"Are we level, Greg?" Steve forced his voice to remain calm. If he came apart now it was the end of everything. And the boy was in bad enough shape. The flight was certain to have kept him on edge, he had a dying man on his hands, and now his father was unconscious from God knew what.

And the pilot was blind. But they had one thing in their favor. Greg lacked the ability to handle the Navion but he *could* act as Steve's eyes and tell him what was going on with the instruments. But above all he had to keep the boy calm, and under tight discipline as well. Steve repeated the question, more firmly this time. "Greg, tell me if we're level. Look at the gyro horizon. The small plane on the gauge. It's—"

"We're slightly nose high, Colonel."

Steve breathed deeply and eased forward on the yoke. "Tell me just *before* we get back to level flight, Greg." That way he could anticipate what was happening and he wouldn't be overcontrolling. His own years of experience and instinct would be another payoff at this moment, as critical as anything he'd ever known. If they were going to survive, he had to keep both himself and the boy cool and as calm as they could manage under the circumstances.

"You're just a few degrees nose high, Colonel."

Steve paused only a moment, then eased back on the yoke. "You're level, sir," came Greg's voice.

That would hold them for the moment. "All right, Greg, you understand the situation, don't you?"

"Uh, sure, yes, sir."

"You're going to have to be my eyes, Greg."

"I understand." Pause. "But . . . my father. What's happened to him?"

"I don't know, Greg. I don't think it's a stroke, or he'd have slumped over. My best guess, son, is that he's got brain pressure of some sort. I'm just guessing. But you've got to understand that the only way we can help your father is to get this thing safely on the ground. You've got to be cool, son."

Greg took a deep breath. "I'll handle it, Colonel. I'll also hold my father back. Off the controls, I mean."

Steve nodded. Flying this way was maddening. A thousand tiny impressions were stabbing through his body and his mind. But he'd flown long enough to know you could *never* trust your seat-of-the-pants impressions when you couldn't see. The balance organs of the ear got false signals. Many pilots couldn't fly on the gauges, without reference to the outside horizon, even when they could see perfectly. He thought of flying by feel, and he knew that that was a guarantee of death for them all. He had no choice but to have the boy see for him. That, and the autopilot. God, he'd almost forgotten about that!

"Greg, listen to me. The autopilot. Can you see it? Do you know where it is?"

"Yes, sir. Just above and to the left of the throttle."

Steve's left hand groped gently. He had it.

"Colonel! We're in a steep bank! To the left! We're going down!"

Gently, carefully, he brought the yoke to the right to correct, came back gently on the yoke to bring up the nose. It was sloppy in this turbulence, but it would do for the moment. "The compass, Greg. The direction gyro. See it?"

"Uh-huh."

"What's our heading?"

"Three three zero."

"All right. I'm going to start coming back to five degrees. Just east of north. Let me know when we're at due north. Better yet, son, call off the headings in ten-degree increments."

He eased the ship back to their course, flying carefully, his hand on the yoke and feet on the rudders damping out the turbulence with practiced ease. He had to get them back on course and then punch in that autopilot.

"Due north, sir."

Steve started to bring them out of the turn. "You're on five degrees now."

"Right. Tell me when my finger is on the activate switch of the autopilot."

"A bit lower, Colonel. There; that's it."

Steve moved the switch. He felt the yoke fight his hand for a moment, and he eased off hand pressure. "The heading lock, Greg."

"Just to the right of the activate switch. You—you're on it now."

Steve stabbed the button. He leaned back in his seat, wiping sweat from his face. The autopilot had them now. Despite the beating they were still taking from the storm, they would hold course and the wings would stay level. That would keep them out of any graveyard spirals with the nose dropping lower and lower while their speed built up to dangerous limits.

"Greg, we've got to try something rough now."

"Yes, sir."

"Watch your feet. I'm moving the front seat back as far as I can. Greg, we're going to have to get your father into the back. I need to get into the left seat up here. Then we'll bring you here with me. Think we can handle it?"

"I sure can try, Colonel."

Steve released his seat belt and fumbled for the belt on the body of the unconscious senator. "That's all I can ask. Okay, let's give it a go."

Sergeant Jill Denby keyed her microphone. "Navion four-three-seven-two kilo from Luke RAPCON. Seven-two kilo, do you read? Over." She turned as Major Phillips came into the control room.

"Where are they?" Phillips asked as he came up to her.

She pointed to the blip on the screen. "Right there, sir. Forty miles out."

"Good," he said, nodding. "Have you talked with them?"

"No, sir." Her face mirrored her frustration. "No response, Major. They just don't answer. Maybe they're not receiving us. They're in heavy weather, sir." Again she gestured to the screen. "Another thing. They've changed course several times. Something strange is going on up there."

They looked at one another.

It seemed to take an eternity to get it done. They heaved and struggled to move one hundred and eighty pounds of inert weight over the backrest of the front seat. Greg half-stood between the legs of the unconscious Lannon, trying to ease his father into the rear seat he had just vacated. In the tight confines of the Navion cabin, without Steve Austin's bionics strength, they might never have made it. But it was done, and as carefully as possible.

"Greg, tighten your father's seat belt. I'm getting into the left seat."

"Yes, sir."

"Then climb up here, boy. I need you."

He felt the movement of Greg coming over the seatback and buckling in. Steve thought for a moment. "Greg, you have sunglasses with you?"

He imagined the look on the boy's face at the question, and the surprise was evident in the tone of his voice. "Why . . . yes, sir."

"All right, Greg. Hold one lens directly beneath your father's nose. Do it now."

He waited a few moments. "All right, Colonel. I'm doing it."

"Look at it quickly, Greg."

"There's . . . there's moisture . . . he's breathing . . . *My God, he's alive, Colonel Austin!*"

"I thought he would be. Okay. Let's get to work."

And it went as well as it could. With the autopilot on, Steve didn't need to make constant corrections to hold the wings level. The autopilot also held them on course. Altitude was another matter. Shifting the two bodies around had changed their balance, but with Greg acting as his eyes, Steve adjusted the trim easily enough to hold their altitude. The Navion swayed and rocked and jolted them about, and Steve would have far preferred to fly the thing himself, but this was safer at the moment.

He had Greg go through the entire panel, reading off to him every gauge, and using the boy as his eyes, Steve had a complete picture of everything that was happening.

"Colonel—"

"What is it?"

"Ahead of us, sir. It looks like some breaks in the clouds."

"That's the best news in a long time, Greg. We've got some other work to do. Our transmitter is out, but we still have VHF. Right?"

"Yes, sir."

"Can you see it?"

"I've got it, Colonel."

"Is it on?"

"Yes, sir."

"I can't hear it. Bring up the volume, Greg. About three-quarters to max."

"Yes, sir. Done." They could hear static crackle from the cabin speakers now.

"All right, Greg. You're doing fine. Can you find the transponder?"

"Yes, sir."

"Is it on?"

"On."

"Dial in the numbers seven seven zero zero."

"Got it, sir."

Steve reached over with his right hand and gently squeezed the young man's arm. "Now, let's hope someone bright is paying attention to a radar scope at Luke."

Jill Denby went rigid in her seat, staring.

"We have a change!" she said, sucking in her breath. "See it? There . . . we have a transponder change. They're squawking emergency. Seven seven hundred code." She turned to Oscar Goldman. "It means they're trying to tell us something, sir. No transmitter."

"Can they receive us?" Goldman pressed.

Her lips tightened. "We'll find out." She turned back

to her console. "Aircraft squawking emergency, this is Luke RAPCON. If you read, please press your ident."

"Now *that* is the most beautiful voice in the world," Steve Austin said with a grin. "Greg, got the ident button?"

"Yes, *sir*. I sure do."

"Then say hello to the lady for us."

"Damn! Look at it!" Cheers broke out from the people in radar control. "Just be-yootiful!"

Jill Denby forced her voice to stay calm, professional.

"Roger, aircraft, we copy your ident. If you are Navion four-three-seven-two kilo, please ident again. Over."

The glowing blip blossomed before their eyes.

"That's *them*, all right!" Oscar Goldman said with a half-shout.

But Jill Denby wasn't listening. "Roger, seven-two kilo. We've been expecting you. Your position is now two-five miles, repeat two-five miles, south of Luke. Turn left to approach heading three four zero."

They watched and waited. The blip shifted ever so slightly from its previous course and steadied on the new course of 340 degrees.

Major Phillips clapped his hand against Goldman's shoulder. "We've got 'em! They're home free!"

CHAPTER FIFTEEN

"Greg, we're doing pretty good now. You understand that?"

"Yes, Colonel." He hesitated. "Anyway, I'm sure glad *you're* telling me that."

Steve couldn't help the chuckle that came from his lips. "You're doing just great. Now, listen to me, boy. When we get closer to the ground you're going to have to give me information a bit faster than we've been doing."

"I'll try my best."

"I know that. Now, I'm going to roll just a bit left and then right, using the autopilot control. I'll move it one notch each way. That's so you'll know just how fast this ship responds that way. And the longer we can stay on the autopilot the better off we are." Steve took a deep breath. "Landing is going to be some kind of game, but if you can keep up with what's happening, and tell me fast enough, we should have it knocked."

"Yes, sir."

"Okay, let's give it a shot. I'll bring in a left turn now." Blinded or not, Steve knew he could turn the Navion with the small control knob of the autopilot. Certainly he couldn't overcontrol using that system, and this would be his last chance to have Greg Hill thoroughly acquaint himself with how the Navion reacted.

"Let me know when we're twenty degrees past three four zero, Greg."

"You're just about there now."

"Okay. I'll stop the turn." He dialed to the right and the wings came level. "Now, we'll crack it a bit the other way." They began a gentle sweeping turn to the right, Greg calling out the numbers, until Steve rolled her out on 340 degrees.

"Okay, Greg. This little dude here," he tapped the autopilot, "can sing and dance, but that's about all. It doesn't hold altitude from what I remember of it. Did we lose or gain any altitude in those turns?"

"Uh, I don't think so, Colonel. We're maybe fifty feet lower than before, but that's all."

"That's good enough. What's it like outside, Greg?"

"We're in the soup again. It's all gray outside. All I can see are our wing tips."

"Well, it gets better the lower we go. Notice how the turbulence has just about died away?"

Greg was startled. "Why . . . you're right, and I never even realized it!"

"Like I say, things just get better. Can you see the fuel gauges?"

"Uh-huh."

"How do they read?"

"Not very good, sir. Maybe an eighth of a tank. It's between a quarter of a tank and empty."

"Both of them?"

"Yes, sir."

"Find me the fuel pump switch, Greg."

Several moments later the lad had what Steve wanted. "Got it."

"Move it to the ON position."

"Yes, sir. It's done."

"Okay. Can you find the gear handle? Don't move it. Just find it and remember where it is."

"Got it."

"Now, the flaps."

"Yes, sir."

"All right, Greg. You keep scanning the gauges. Tell

142

me if anything seems to be wrong. Even if a gauge suddenly shows something different, let me know."

"Will do, Colonel."

"Good man. Now," Steve said with a deep breath, "we can tell the people on the ground the *bad* news."

His hand reached forward. "Put my finger on the ident button, on the transponder," he told Greg.

"You've got it now, sir."

"Great." Steve began pressing the ident rapidly in a series of intermittent bursts.

"Colonel, I don't understand. What's that you're doing?"

"Talking, I hope," came the reply.

Oscar Goldman came slowly from his seat as the glowing blip on the radar scope started to flash on and off. "What's wrong?" he demanded, his voice sharper than he'd intended. "Why is that blip flashing like that?"

"I—I don't know," Jill Denby said, as puzzled as the others. Suddenly her face brightened. "Wait . . . I recognize it now . . . It's Morse! Morse code!"

She spoke quickly into her mike. "Seven-two kilo, Luke RAPCON." She was reaching for a pen and pad as she talked. "If you're transmitting Morse through your code ident, please begin your transmissions again. We are ready to copy. Over."

Steve's finger pressed again and again. The electronic signals flashed through space, appearing as tiny blossoms of light miles from the approaching Navion.

They hovered over Sergeant Jill Denby as she marked off the dots and dashes of the Morse code signal, writing against each series of dah-dit flashes the equivalent letter.

PILOT
AUSTIN
BLINDED

"Blinded?" Goldman's voice was nearly a shout. "What the hell is going on up there? I thought Hill was a pilot!" He shook his head, anger and frustration mixed on his face. "Ask him about Hill," he ordered the girl.

"Seven-two kilo, Luke RAPCON. What is the condition of General Hill?"

The blips blossomed one after the other.

HILL

UNCONSCIOUS

AUSTIN

FLYING

"But he said he was *blind!*" Goldman cried.

The blossoms of light continued.

PASSENGER

ASSISTING

Major Phillips leaned forward. "Sergeant, don't waste any time. He'll do what he can. Fly him in."

She nodded. She was as stunned and shaken as the others with her, but *she* was on that mike and reading the console, and *she*—not anyone else—would have to bring down that blinded man. She took a deep breath and forced calm upon herself.

"Roger, seven-two kilo. Understand your message. Colonel Austin is blind and a passenger will assist you in approach and landing. If you copy, give me one long ident, please."

The light blossomed, held its brilliance, then went out.

"Very good, seven-two kilo. We will initiate precision radar approach. If you do not understand or cannot comply with instructions, give us three fast idents. Confirm now with one long ident, please."

Another long blossom of light.

"Seven-two kilo, you are now twelve miles south. That is one-two miles south. Begin descent to two thousand."

A single blossom of light.

Jill Denby sagged in her seat with relief. "He's reading us loud and clear," she said, as much to herself as the others. There was nothing else for her to do at this moment except to wait—and watch.

Behind her Major Phillips grabbed a phone.

"Major Phillips here," he barked into the mouthpiece. "We have a mayday. Move the crash trucks and emergency medical teams to the far end of runway thirty-two. It's a civilian aircraft and the pilot is blind. We're trying to talk him down, so be ready for anything. Got it? Then *move!*"

In the cabin of the Navion, Steve Austin prepared to fly with a delicate touch he'd never before brought to an airplane. He hoped that "touch of delicate" would continue all the way to the ground. Whatever he did now must be an exquisite blend of his own experience and skill, his ability to translate what he could feel, the swiftness and the reality of translating what he heard from Greg, and transferring all that information to what needed to be done.

"Greg, the autopilot will keep the wings level and hold us on course. Understand that?"

The teenager swallowed hard, nodding even before he realized the other man couldn't see him. "Yes, sir. Got it."

"All right. A lot depends upon your ability to be my eyes, to crawl inside my head with what you see. I'm going to come back on the power. I want you to watch the rate of descent—do you know where that instrument is? Good. Also, our altitude, as it changes. And our airspeed. Keep reading off the numbers from those gauges." Steve took a deep breath. "Here we go, fella . . ."

His right hand grasped the throttle knob, his forefinger extended against the panel. He eased back on the control, then hesitated. "Greg, the manifold pressure gauge—"

"I see it, Colonel."

"Let me know when I've backed off to eighteen inches pressure."

"Right. Keep going."

The throttle eased back. "Twenty-one, twenty . . . uh . . . you're at eighteen now, Colonel Austin."

145

"Good. What's our airspeed?"

"It's . . . showing 110."

"Fine. Now the rate of descent."

"Seven . . . uh . . . no, it's 800 feet a minute."

"Great. Call off altitude changes every 500 feet."

"Yes, sir. Uh, Colonel Austin, we're descending at twelve hundred feet a minute."

"Good man," Steve said quickly. He groped for the trim wheel, felt gently to be sure what he had under his fingers, and rolled in nose-up trim to slow their descent rate. Several moments later Greg announced the results.

"Eight hundred feet a minute, Colonel. And we're holding steady as a rock."

"We have good track on you, seven-two kilo." Jill Denby's voice came through the cabin's speakers sharp and crisp. *"You are nine miles southeast and coming through two thousand. Turn left to three zero zero and begin a standard rate descent. You are clear for GCA approach, to runway three two. Wind is calm, visibility one mile. You will break through the overcast at seven hundred feet above ground level. Please start your turn to three zero zero."*

Steve cursed to himself. He heard, he felt, the roughness in the engine. He'd forgotten—"Greg, the mixture control. The red handle. Push it all the way forward." He felt the youngster move by his side. "It's in," Greg said, and even as Steve heard the words the engine smoothed out. He'd forgotten that at altitude they'd been flying with the mixture leaned out. God, they could have lost this whole thing if he hadn't come to his senses.

"Read them off," he said to Greg.

"Coming down at seven hundred feet a—"

"Too fast," Steve broke in. He didn't want to use any more nose-up trim. He fed in more power. When he thought about power he made his decision. "Greg, the prop control. Put my hand on it." When he felt the control beneath his hand, he moved it forward. The propeller went to flat pitch and maximum RPM. They'd have better power response now when he advanced the

146

throttle, and it was one less thing to worry about later.

"We're at 500 feet a minute now, Colonel."

"Speed and altitude, Greg."

"Uh, ninety. But it's getting lower. It's eighty-five now, and—"

Steve didn't wait. He nudged the throttle, listened to Greg call off the speed as it increased. He was satisfied with an even hundred miles an hour.

The woman's voice came sweetly to him.

"*Seven-two kilo, you are now seven miles from the runway. Come right to three two zero, please.*"

He had his hand on the autopilot knob. "Call the numbers, Greg." He eased the knob to the side. The autopilot handled it like silk.

"Coming up on three twenty. Hold it—"

"*You are on course, seven-two kilo. You are descending below glide path. Decrease your rate of descent.*"

More power. Then . . . wait.

"*You are coming back to glide path. Continue your correction.*" A long pause. "*You are on glide path. Seven-two kilo, you are five miles from the runway. Continue your approach.*"

"We're on the button, Colonel Austin."

Steve nodded in his darkness.

"*Seven-two kilo, four miles from the runway, twelve hundred feet above the ground. Looking good. Come left five degrees.*" The long pause; then: "*On glide path, continue descent. How about your gear, seven-two kilo?*"

A long blossom of light to confirm he'd heard.

"Okay, Greg. Got the gear handle? Down it goes, boy."

"Yes, *sir*."

They heard and felt the gear coming into position. "Call me the green lights, son."

"Yes, sir. Three in the green, just like my dad calls them out."

"Good. We'll—"

"*Seven-two kilo, suggest you add power. You are dropping below the glide path. You are—*"

147

Steve wasn't waiting. He brought in more throttle, trying to judge what pitch change he'd need with the trim. They were porpoising now as he followed the movements of the Navion, instead of being able to anticipate them.

"Altitude, Greg."

"Nine hundred feet, sir. But our speed is coming down. It's at seventy-five now, and—"

The throttle went forward some more. Steve fed in nose-down trim, just a hair.

"Eighty, eighty-five, coming up on ninety."

"Jesus, that's better."

"*Seven-two kilo, you are two miles from the runway at eight hundred feet. You should break out into the clear any moment now.*"

Steve added more power. "Descent rate," he snapped.

"Four hundred feet, Colonel."

More power, a touch of trim change. Then: "Greg, I want three-quarter flaps. You know where the handle is. Can you find the flap indicator on the panel?"

"Got it."

"Okay. Be ready to call out any sudden change in speed or anything else. Start 'em down, and stop them moving just before the three-quarter position."

"All right, Colonel. They're coming down now."

Steve flew by feel, sounds, the rumble of the airplane, adding power to compensate for the drag of the flaps. "Call 'em out," he told the youth.

"Three hundred feet a minute descent, airspeed eighty-five, altitude about seven hundred fifty."

"Okay. When we break out of this stuff, I'm going on the controls myself. When I tell you, I want you to disconnect the autopilot. When that happens, Greg, you've got to talk to me just about every second, keep me pointed to the runway. Set?"

"Yes, sir."

Jill Denby pulled the microphone closer to her lips. "Seven-two kilo, expect any moment to break out of the overcast. You are on course, on glide path. Continue

148

your approach. When you have the field in sight, give us a long ident, please."

She stared at the scope and less than twenty seconds later the light blossomed again.

"Very good, seven-two kilo. You are cleared to land. No further transmissions." She hesitated, then added softly, "Good luck, sir."

Behind her Oscar Goldman was stunned with her words. He stepped back, dragging Major Phillips with him. He whispered fiercely in his ear. "What the hell is she doing? What's this no further transmission nonsense? How the hell is he going to get down!"

"Easy, easy, Mr. Goldman. They've got the runway in sight. They're eyeballing it now and the man in that plane can react faster than anything we can do to help him from here."

"But he's blind, dammit!"

"The passenger with him has eyes," Phillips said quickly. "He'll be talking Colonel Austin down all the way."

Goldman stared at him, still not believing what he was hearing. "I hope to God you're right, Major," he snapped, and turned back to the radar scope.

"Got the runway in sight?"

"Yes, sir, and it sure looks good, Colonel."

Steve gripped the yoke with his left hand and kept his right on the throttle, his feet on the rudder pedals. "All right. Autopilot *off*."

"It's off, Colonel."

Steve felt the transition as the yoke came alive. "Don't stop talking, Greg."

"Yes, sir. Our sped is eighty-five, altitude six hundred, and we're coming down at just under three hundred feet a minute."

"We need a tad more power," Steve murmured. "Let me know when we're at two hundred a minute coming down." He increased power, came back on the trim to hold the nose up.

"Call 'em," he cracked.

"Speed between eighty and eighty-five. Descent at two fifty. We're just under six hundred feet." Greg peered through the windshield. "Uh, you're drifting just a bit to the left, Colonel. Better come around to the right."

"Okay, son. Very good. I'm going to use some heavy rudder in here. The less I bank this thing the better. It'll be sloppy, but it works. Let me know when we're lined up again."

Greg watched. "You're in the groove, sir."

Steve eased off the foot pressure.

"Just keep on trucking, Colonel."

"We'll do just that," Steve agreed. "Now, let me know when we're approaching the runway. I want to cross the end with some height. You keep me lined up and let me know when we're about ten feet up, okay?"

"Yes, sir. I've watched my dad before. I think I can judge it pretty good."

"Fine. Just at that point, I'll come back on power and the yoke at the same time so she settles. Just point me down that big concrete stretch."

"Uh, yes, sir. Better come right some more."

Steve corrected. "Okay. Make sure our speed doesn't get below eighty-five at any point until we're over the end of the field. Got it?"

"Yes, sir. We're coming down now at two hundred feet a minute. Better bring in some more power. Our speed is dropping a bit."

Steve advanced the throttle. "Make it ninety, Greg. I want some money in the bank."

"Uh, okay. You're still lined up neatly. Speed is ninety, but we're holding altitude."

Steve would rather bring her in hot than drop his speed and mess around with a stall. He eased forward on the yoke. "Just about a hundred for speed, Colonel."

"Piece of cake," Steve murmured. "Keep talking, Greg."

"You're lined up. Descent is about two fifty, speed at one hundred, and we're coming up on the field now. I think we're a little hot, Colonel."

"That's a lot of concrete out there," Steve reassured him.

"Come right some more."

He used the rudder again. Let her be sloppy. No one was passing more than one kind of test right now. Survival.

"That's it. We're coming right down the groove. The end of the field is right in front of us now . . . keep her going, we're a bit high, we're lined up, we've just passed the end of the runway, Colonel!"

Steve came back on power, slowly, steadily.

"You're drifting left . . . good, good. We're over the center line, holding just right, that's perfect, Colonel, I think we're about ten feet up now, we're—"

Steve wasn't waiting. He came back some more on the throttle, keeping in just enough power to let her fly with some authority, bringing the nose back with the yoke.

"Ninety, coming down on the speed, eighty-five, eighty, we're at seventy-five, we're almost there, we—"

Steve felt the tires touch concrete. Instantly he chopped all power.

"Come right! We're drifting—"

He shoved forward on the yoke, getting the nose wheel down solidly, slamming on brake pressure. He heard rubber squealing in protest.

"Come right!"

He eased off on the left brake. He could feel the Navion dumping its speed, solid on the ground. There was a sudden bump, a jolt, and then they stopped moving.

"I think we hit a runway light, Colonel."

"How about that?" Steve said with a huge grin. "Get your hand on the mixture control, Ace. Got it? Bring it all the way back now."

Moments later the engine coughed and shook itself into silence. "Can you find the mag switches? Turn them to OFF."

"It's done, sir."

"One last thing, Ace. The master switch."

151

"Uh-huh. It's off."

"Open that damn canopy. Fresh air would sure taste good."

He felt the boy tugging, heard the scrape of the canopy sliding back. Cool air washed over them in blessed relief, and they heard the scream of approaching sirens.

"Out of sight, Colonel, *you did it*," Greg said proudly.

"No way, Ace," Steve insisted. "We, *and* a sweet voice in Luke RAPCON, did it."

CHAPTER SIXTEEN

Steve Austin took hold of the elastic band, shifted aside the patch over his eye, and walked to the window of his hospital room. It was all there. He could see. Not as clearly as in the past. But certainly better than the cloudy view of the night before.

He stared across Luke Air Force Base at the shadows of a new day. The longer he looked, the sharper the images came into focus. The blackness of night had diminished to pools of concentrated brightness. He breathed deeply. So had his own darkness. God, it was great to see. Man has no other gift more important, he thought quietly, enjoying sights as if he'd never seen them before—a morning sun bouncing its rays off the polished metal flanks of a row of sweptwing jets.

His solitude was interrupted by the sound of someone entering the room. He turned to face Oscar Goldman.

"Morning, Steve. How's the eye? Any problems?"

"Morning, Oscar," he nodded, reaching for his jacket. "Not now. I was just checking it out. I'm as good as new."

"Good. They told me you were a lucky man." Goldman smiled. "I see you're ready to get out of here."

"Just about. Waiting for the Doc to give me the nod," Steve answered. "He's on his way by to give me his okay."

"Good," Oscar said, gesturing toward the door. "I have a driver waiting to take us to our plane and—"

"Hey, Oscar," Steve broke in, puzzled. "Aren't you forgetting that little matter with the Board of Inquiry?"

"No, not at all," he shook his head. "I have some good news about that."

"Such as?"

"You're off the hook," Oscar smiled again. "There'll be no inquiry. General Hill has agreed to retire and accept full responsibility for the VC-135 crash."

"How about the Senate?"

"Oh, he'd like to finish his term," Oscar said, "but with his problem . . . uh . . . well—"

"Any ideas on what his problem is?" Steve interrupted quietly, sitting down on the bed.

"A few suspicions," Oscar told him, pulling up a chair. "I was talking with some of the doctors yesterday after they brought Hill in, and the evidence points toward an astrocytoma of the temporal lobe."

"A what?"

"It's a slow-growing tumor, Steve. The way I understand it, it may grow for four to six years before detection."

"Well, how in the hell did they come up with that so damn fast?"

"They didn't," Oscar said. "It seems Senator Hill consulted a specialist some months ago who suspected the tumor and he told the boys here about it last night."

"Uh-huh, and this thing causes a person to black out?"

"Well, no, not exactly," Oscar explained. "The symptoms are, when a person suffers an attack from an astrocytoma tumor, he first begins misnaming objects, having difficulty using common words. He just sits in a dreamy trance."

"He was in a trance, all right," Steve said, "a rigid trance. We could hardly move him."

"So I understand," Oscar nodded. "And according to the doctors, he could have been perfectly comfortable in his own mind. Enjoying a daydream which, the way

154

I understand it, becomes completely real to him; a mirage, what they call the *déjà vu* phenomenon, the feeling of having experienced at some prior time something actually being experienced for the first time. In other words a psychic fit."

"Is it curable?"

"Well, first they must determine if in fact it is an astrocytoma," Oscar answered. "If it is, its stage of growth. If——"

"But no more flying, right?"

"Right."

"That's good," Steve said. "Too bad he waited until now to face his problem. If he hadn't," he shrugged, "Tom Jeffers and three other good airmen would be alive to——"

"Hey, buddy," Goldman came back at him. "Twenty-twenty hindsight, you know. The man wasn't aware of——"

"Hell, I'm not the man's judge, Oscar. We're all guilty as hell when it comes to holding on, protecting what we feel is important to us and to those we love."

"Right, Steve," Oscar agreed. "Who's to say——"

Goldman broke into his own words as both of them turned their attention to the doorway. A man in surgical green came into the room.

"Good morning, Colonel," the man said, taking a penlight from his pocket. "How's the eye?"

"Fine, Major. Not a hundred per cent, but fine."

The doctor tugged at the eye patch Steve had shifted to his forehead. "The light doesn't bother you?" he asked.

"No, not all that much."

"Good," the doctor said, leaning forward, pointing the beam of the penlight directly into Steve's eye.

A moment later he snapped off the light and stood erect. "As they say, Colonel, a clean bill of health," he said, adding quickly, "thanks to that boy. What he did —cleansing the eye, keeping the light out of it, well, you owe your sight to him."

"I know it, Doc."

"Uh, sorry I couldn't help you with your other eye," the doctor said. "It's too advanced. Way out of my line."

"That's all right, Doctor," Oscar spoke up. "We have a specialist in mind. Thank you, anyway."

"I'm sure you do, Mr. Goldman." The doctor grinned. "That's one fine piece of engineering. Could I ask—"

"No, Major," Oscar said firmly. "But we do appreciate all you did for Colonel Austin."

"I understand," the doctor said, turning back to Steve. "Well, Colonel, you're free to go as soon as you take care of one little thing for me."

"What's that, Doctor?"

"Your autograph for my two sons," he smiled.

"My pleasure, sir. What are their names?"

"Brian and Daniel Gibbons."

Steve reached for a piece of hospital stationery on the table beside the bed and began to write. "Doctor, how's Mr. Lannon this morning?"

"He's resting comfortably, Colonel. Again thanks to that Hill youngster. He's right up to date on snakebite procedure."

"I have a feeling Greg Hill is right up to date on many things," Steve said, handing the sheet of paper to the major. "Give my best to your sons, Doctor Gibbons," he added as they walked from the room.

Steve and Oscar Goldman reached the hospital's waiting room to find Senator Ed Hill sitting in a wheelchair, dressed in hospital pajamas and robe, Greg by his side.

"Colonel." Hill smiled broadly. "Can I shake your hand before you go?"

Steve stopped before the wheelchair and extended his hand. "Certainly, General."

"Oh, no, not General, not Senator. None of them any more." He shook his head. "Just old Ed Hill, lucky to be alive." He paused. "Thank you."

"No, don't thank me, thank *him*," Steve said, nodding

toward Greg. "We all owe your son a great deal, General."

"Oh, I have the rest of my life to repay him, but you I may never see again. And you're a very special man, Colonel," he said with a wink. "The best thing I ever did was to get Oscar that six million."

"No, General," Steve disagreed again. "The best thing you ever did was to raise a son." He turned, extending his hand to Greg. "Goodbye, *Ace*," he smiled. "We'll have to do it again someday."

"Right, someday." Greg returned his smile and shook his hand. "Goodbye, Colonel."

"Steve," Oscar said as he gestured toward the door, "you go on ahead. Our car and driver are right outside. I have a couple of things to go over with the senator."

"Right, understand, Oscar," he said with a final wave as he turned and started for the door.

He'd taken only a few steps across the waiting room when he came face to face with a pretty WAF.

"Colonel Austin?"

"Yes, that's right."

"I thought so," the young woman said shyly. "We've never met, exactly, but, well, I just couldn't let you leave without saying hello. I'm Sergeant Denby."

Steve stared at her neatly pressed uniform. He was puzzled but not all that surprised. Since he'd returned from the moon, he'd been approached many times by people who simply wanted to introduce themselves. But, somehow, this was different. Perhaps the voice, he thought. Finally he said, "Nice to meet you, Sergeant."

"Well . . . uh . . . are you all right now?" Jill asked awkwardly.

"Yes, I think so," he answered. "Nice of you to—" He broke into his own words. "Sergeant, you sure we haven't met somewhere before?"

"No, sir, not really," Jill said, backing away. "If you'll excuse me, Colonel Austin, I've got to get over

157

to RAPCON. I just wanted to be sure you were all right," she added, turning for the door.

Steve nodded as he watched the young woman leave. RAPCON . . . RAPCON, he thought. Suddenly his face brightened. That's it, Austin, you thick-headed . . .

"Hey, Sergeant!" he shouted, his bionics legs driving him through the door in swift pursuit of Jill Denby.

His abrupt departure captured the immediate attention of everyone in the waiting room. They moved to the window to see Steve Austin catch up to the young WAF. They saw him pantomine flying and point to her. She nodded vigorously and his arms encircled her, sweeping her off her feet. They all smiled at the sight of a Colonel kissing a Sergeant. It was *not* one of your everyday sights.

MORE ADVENTURES OF STEVE AUSTIN
IN THESE EXCITING BOOKS!

CYBORG by Martin Caidin   **(76-643, $1.25)**
A National Bestseller! Is he man or machine? He was born
human. After the accident NASA put him back together with 6
million dollars worth of electronic parts. He can do anything
any man can do—except love.

THE SIX MILLION DOLLAR MAN #1: WINE, WOMEN & WARS
Michael Jahn   **(76-833, $1.25)**
Steve Austin fights an international bandit who steals nuclear
weapons. His job is to locate this madman before he accom-
plishes his most daring piracy.

THE SIX MILLION DOLLAR MAN #2:   **(76-834, $1.25)**
THE SOLID GOLD KIDNAPPING
by Evan Richards
Steve Austin challenges an international ring that specializes
in kidnapping political figures.

SIX MILLION DOLLAR MAN #3:   **(76-408, $1.25)**
HIGH CRYSTAL
by Martin Caidin
A fast-paced novel that combines the appeal of the scientific
superman with the **Chariots of the Gods** mystique. An original
novel which appeared in hardback and won critical applause.

W A Warner Communications Company

Please send me the books I have checked.

Enclose check or money order only, no cash please. Plus 25¢
per copy to cover postage and handling. N.Y. State residents
add applicable sales tax.

Please allow 2 weeks for delivery.

WARNER PAPERBACK LIBRARY
P.O. Box 690
New York, N.Y. 10019

Name ....

Address ....

City .... State .... Zip ....

_____ Please send me your free mail order catalog

GREAT SCIENCE FICTION FROM WARNER PAPERBACK LIBRARY!

THE FRANKENSTEIN FACTORY   (76-861, $1.25)
by Edward D. Hoch
Yesterday's horror story becomes tomorrow's reality as a team of doctors creates a new man from parts of dead men cryogenically frozen years before.

THE DRACULA TAPE   (78-869, $1.50)
by Fred Saberhagen
With an attention to the details of the original Dracula story, and an amazing knowledge of historical and literary Vampirana, Saberhagen writes this fang-in-cheek adventure in a style that will delight vampire fans and others.

WHEN WORLDS COLLIDE   (76-881, $1.25)
by Philip Wylie & Edwin Balmer
Two outlaw planets are going to collide with Earth! Scientists begin to build rockets to evacuate "the chosen few" to a distant planet to start anew—but word gets out. Mass hysteria brings out the worst, as people fight for survival.

AFTER WORLDS COLLIDE   (76-873, $1.25)
by Philip Wylie & Edwin Balmer
The classic sequel to **When Worlds Collide.** When a group of survivors landed on Bronson Beta they expected absolute desolation. Instead they found a beautiful city—and also found that they were not alone.

 A Warner Communications Company

Please send me the books I have checked.

Enclose check or money order only, no cash please. Plus 25¢ per copy to cover postage and handling. N.Y. State residents add applicable sales tax.

Please allow 2 weeks for delivery.

WARNER PAPERBACK LIBRARY
P.O. Box 690
New York, N.Y. 10019

Name ....

Address ....

City .... State .... Zip ....
_____ Please send me your free mail order catalog